HUBRIS

The Chronicles of a Tooth Fairy

HUBRIS

The Chronicles of a Tooth Fairy

Part 1

Georgiea Howarth

Hubris

The Chronicles of a Tooth Fairy

For Axel,

&

my fairy Queen, and King.
Without you, this world would not exist.

Since the waking of the earth,
there have always been, the others.
You should know,
all the tales ever told around the fireside,
every bedtime story whispered in the night,
they are all true.
Somewhere between the light and the dark,
in places out of reach of man, live the others,
The hardest working of all the others,
is the Tooth Fairy.

*

Always clean your teeth, before you go to bed.

*

Before.

'Guilty!'

'Guilty my lord!'

'Aye, guilty as well.'

'This council finds the accused, guilty as charged, of hubris, rebellious sedition, and cruelty towards a human child. Your Majesty, the sentence must be carried out swiftly. With regards to your position in this matter, we will allow you time to compose yourself. There is no alternative Nemesia, you must take her wings.'

*

Far below the council chamber, Marguerite pressed her forehead against the icy metal of the cell door. The searing cold stabbed into her temples. Heart pounding, her hands began to tremble again.

'You have to listen to me!' hissed Blossom. From outside she whispered through the lock. 'The council has made a ruling; she really means to do it. Marguerite, we have to get you out.'

'Just leave Blossom, there is nothing you can do,' she replied gruffly, the words catching in her throat.

'Yes! Yes, there is,' urged Blossom. 'I have a plan; I can get a keyhole.'

'No, Blossom, just go.'

'I have to, this is my fault as well. I should have looked after you, taught you better.'

'No,' insisted Marguerite. Deep as her own misery was, Marguerite knew her friend did not understand. Blossom thought that this was somehow her fault. She knew nothing about the elves, and still thought this was about taking the teeth from that silly child. 'Blossom, listen. Listen to me, this is about more than just the teeth, you have to go, there is nothing you can do…'

'I can.'

'I don't need your help!' Marguerite shouted at the door.

Somewhere in the chambers above them a horn sounded, the melodious call echoing throughout the palace. Startled, Blossom looked nervously about the shadowy corridors. 'I have to go, but I promise, I won't let you down Marguerite…' her voice faded.

'What… Blossom, stop,' called Marguerite. She strained to hear her friend through the lock. 'Blossom? Blossom…' Falling to her knees, Marguerite covered her face with quivering hands.

Ice melted, on the ceiling water dripped from the light caged by metal wires into a puddle on the cell floor. Marguerite counted each drop aloud, trying to ignore the loud thudding of her heart. An hour passed, her voice rasped and shook as she whispered the tally to herself.

The cell door was wrenched open without warning. Shocked, Marguerite staggered to her feet. Guards filled the doorway. Stepping inside they lined the walls, forcing her to the very centre of the room, each of them studiously avoiding her glare.

'So many of you, just for me,' said Marguerite, her pointy chin raised haughtily. 'I'm amazed they didn't send for Linden.'

'They did!' A husky reply came from beyond the open door. The guards snapped to attention as their prince entered, so tall his silver white braids almost brushed the ceiling.

Standing close, he looked down into her frightened, dirty face. 'Marguerite, what were you thinking? To speak with the elves like that, to encourage them to defy Vorgen. After everything we have worked for, the years of negotiation. Good people died to bring this world in order, to create balance amongst our races. You have no idea how very disappointed your mother and I are.'

In the presence of her father, she lost her edge, blushing as the room became uncomfortably warm. 'I didn't mean to,' she said. 'It…it just happened. Can you stop her?'

'No, no more than I could stop the world from turning. You have brought us all dangerously close to a rebellion Marguerite. She must make an example of you, to be lenient now would mean our people losing faith in her.' His uncompromising face infuriated Marguerite. She had expected him to understand, or at least stand up for her with the council.

'Of course, she does! She has to do this to save face. Her throne is more important than I am!' she said.

'Don't be a child Marguerite!' replied Linden sternly. Her adoring, indulgent father was gone, suddenly she saw the prince her people respected. 'Vorgen executed his elves last night. Did you think this was a game?' Marguerite gasped, trembling, her legs almost buckled beneath her.

'You know, I have always defended you Marguerite, but it is time you paid for your behaviour.' Linden lifted a thin black rope from his belt, his eyes holding hers. 'I promised that I would be the one to bind you.'

'Wait…' she cried out. 'You're going to bind me? No! I won't fight, please…please.' Wildly she backed into the guards, 'No you can't!' Strong hands held her firmly to the ground.

'Be brave Marguerite.'

*

Panting, Marguerite lay on the tiled floor at the centre of the Great Hall, the rope loose about her neck. Powerless to lift her head, the damp boots of the guard was all she could see. Angry tears seeped between her lashes, unable to wipe them away, she seethed with embarrassment.

Huge wooden doors swung open; air swept over her in a rush. From outside she could hear excited, angry voices of a crowd in the hallway, silenced as the doors slammed to a close.

'Unbind the prisoner.'

'Your majesty, it would be unwise,' advised the guard.

'I said unbind her, I will speak with my daughter.'

'As you wish.'

The rope slithered from her neck, air flooded back into her lungs, Marguerite scrambled to her knees. 'I won't beg,' she cried.

'I do hope not!' Nemesia, Queen of the Fairies, looked down upon the dirty tooth fairy hunched before her. 'Cruelty, Marguerite?' she said. 'It is a lot less funny now we are here isn't it?'

'I think that might have been exaggerated.'

'You stole his teeth. What we do is a sacred trust. That child will never believe again, not without fear. Is that what you want, for humans to fear us?' asked Nemesia sternly.

'Well, no….' Marguerite cringed.

'No?' asked Nemesia.' However, you do think we should rule this world. What was it you said?' Nemesia paced furiously. 'We should be in charge. They should be hiding from us! Why should we creep about, hiding from them, when we have so much power?'

'It wasn't like that, I told them.' Marguerite squirmed. 'I was just saying that we should….'

'Oh Marguerite, at least have the courage of your convictions,' snapped Nemesia. 'Next, you will be telling me it was Jürgen and the other elves, and that you were not even there.'

'I never said that!' raged Marguerite. 'I am not a baby; I know what I did. But why should we have to serve them? Why, should we make life easier for humans, when they hardly know or care if we exist! Have you ever known a human to be grateful for anything we do? They grab all the goodness, moan about even the tiniest things. Stupid, crude beings, they

14

ruin everything with their clumsy lives. Lazy, greedy, selfish....' Nemesia held up a hand to silence Marguerite. 'Don't think I'm going to shut up, just because you wave a royal hand. You are doing this to save face. You are going to punish me, because I've made you look weak!'

'Is this why, because you want to hurt me?' asked Nemesia.

'You've never had any time for me,' hissed Marguerite. 'Always running after humans, fixing things that were their fault, mistakes that they made. It is different now though. You don't leave her. You never make her wait until you have finished, 'royal' business.'

'Do not tell me, you are jealous of your sister.' Nemesia closed her eyes in despair.

'I am not!' Marguerite leapt to her feet, wings flickering angrily. Instantly the guards surrounded them, cutting her off from the queen, black ropes held out ready to bind her again.

'Enough!' Nemesia waved the guards aside. Her luminous eyes glowing as she struggled to steady her voice. 'Blood was spilt over this. Vorgen executed the first elves in three generations. He took his only child's head, all because you are jealous of Asta.' Marguerite gasped as Nemesia closed long fingers around her arm in an iron grip. 'Look, watch your mischief!'

Marguerite's eyes clouded; a milky glow slid across her pupils. Icy night stung inside her brain. She saw fire torches, the thin terrified faces of four elves kneeling before Vorgen, their king. She smelt damp fur and the crowd surrounding her. A knot tightened in her throat as she met the pale green eyes of the elven queen. Eyes that flashed with the light of a sword as it swung. A heart song grew from an anguished wail, slowly taken up and chanted by all about her. The smell of blood. In the snow, Jürgen, his shocked face stared at the stars with blank eyes. Vorgen raised his sword again. Marguerite gagged, she felt her mother's guilt and pain flood into her chest.

The vision stopped suddenly; Nemesia flung her arm away. 'Yes, their actions were their own. However, the thoughts behind it, they started with you. There is nothing more I can say to you, I only hope that you come to terms with yourself.' Nemesia turned away.

'Why? What are you going to do to me?' asked Marguerite. Sweat started to roll down her sides, shaking, her knees weak.

'We do not execute fairies Marguerite, however much you desire the drama!' said Nemesia. 'You shall be everything that we are not. No more will you possess the power that is a tooth fairy's privilege. Hubris is a great crime; you shall have neither youth nor beauty. Freedom and choice are no longer your right. You will be that which you fear most and shall

16

serve as a warning to all humans who stray. *''He 'ad –a ... jas`amwa, heyyay'''* Nemesia chanted ancient words.

'I'd rather die!' shouted Marguerite in defiance. The guards stepped back. Around her the rune- tiles across the floor glowed, heating the air. Sparks appeared flickering upwards from the red-hot symbols. Marguerite could feel a prickle in her wings, 'No …don't do this! Kill me, not this!'

'''*Lahabla … hes`am*'' ....' Nemesia opened her arms wide. Above her the ceiling blazed with golden light. Ribbons of white-hot fire snaked across the floor toward Marguerite, collecting into a web of searing pinpricks that arched together, forcing her to her knees. '''*S`ama*'' ...' Marguerite gritted her jaws, determined not to scream. '''*Labbava, tala`alu*'' ... ' The lights met, exploding, tearing into her crouched body at the centre of the floor.

'Kill me!'

The scream broke free from her burning silhouette, echoing dreadfully throughout the palace. The crowd in the hallway froze. When a single tear trickled down her face, Nemesia let it splash onto the scorching tiles. She watched as the charred remains of her daughter thudded to the floor.

Outside the hall, other fairies found Blossom. Her unconscious body limp on the ground, the keyhole she had stolen, still open to the dreadful scene in the Great Hall.

*

A warm breeze floated gently across Marguerite. Hair softly tickled her cheek. With great effort, she passed a heavy hand over her face to remove the irritation. Her mouth tasted of iron. Every inch of her skin ached. Opening bruised eyes, Marguerite groaned. Blue light, too bright, made her squint quickly. Maybe she was dead? She pondered this thought.

A silver light flashed in the blue. Was it on her eye? Flexing her fingers, she gasped in pain as her skin tightened. She tried blinking, the all-encompassing blue would not budge, and the shiny thing was still there. Marguerite noticed she was lying down. The surface she was lying on felt hard, warm, but hard. In fact, it was very hard. The noise of the aircraft passing overhead, drowned out the wretched sound as Marguerite realised, she no longer possessed wings.

That night, the enormous nose that now graced her face, sniffed out the first of the dirty teeth. Dragged to their bedsides, in she flew through countless windows changing all the teeth that were not clean, until dawn. When the rest of the world awoke that morning, she was already there, deep in their minds, it was as if she

had always been. They knew her as Granny Green
Teeth.

Sometime after.

'Now Ruby, show me those lovely new teeth,' coaxed the dentist.

'Argh'

Felix Van Doore watched as Ruby, his monstrous baby sister, opened her mouth wide. Sharp, sparkly, new teeth flashed before Mr Fogg; but as he went to reach them, Ruby snapped her mouth closed catching the end of his glove.

'Grr…'growled Ruby, her chubby little face pink and determined.

'Oh no, Ruby. Let go darling,' said Mum. Felix smirked. Ruby hung on tight as the glove stretched greatly between the dentist and his tiny patient.

'Grr, grr.' Ruby did let go. With a rubbery snap, the stretched glove rapped smartly on his finger. Wincing, Mr Fogg picked up a small long handled mirror from the tray.

'Alright, let's try again shall we.'

Grinning out of the window, Felix was careful not to let Mum see. If she saw that he found Ruby amusing, then they would all have to do something 'fun' together. He didn't want to spend more time with the toddler than was necessary. As far as Felix was concerned, any time, was way too much time spent with the frilly, pink, nightmare, of two years and three months, that was his sister.

'Your turn young man,' called Mr Fogg brightly. Felix, determined to be a model patient in comparison to Ruby, settled into the chair, mouth opened wide. 'Wonderful, wonderful,' said Mr Fogg, eyes roving over Felix's teeth. They were strangely larger through his steel-rimmed glasses, magnified to seek out even the smallest imperfection. Felix idled away the seconds staring at the red veins, grey iris, and hugely bushy brows in front of him. 'Marvellous,' declared the dentist. 'I don't know how you do it, but there isn't a blemish to be found.' He only just managed to keep the disappointment out of his voice. Mum blushed under the praise.

'Oh, you know, cleaning twice a day,' said Mum. She hoisted Ruby to her hip. 'Never go to bed without cleaning them thoroughly, we all know what happens if you don't.' She shepherded Felix into the empty reception. Following swiftly, Mr Fogg strode around the reception desk, casually flipping open the appointments book.

'When can we expect to see these two again?' asked Mr Fogg innocently.

'Not for another year I suppose,' Mum strapped Ruby into the buggy.

'I haven't seen Mr Van Doore for some time,' persisted the dentist. Ruby made a bid for freedom, which was hastily subdued.

'Well, you know him. Sylvia's day off is it?' asked Mum

'Erm.' Mr Fogg twiddled with a pen. 'I'm afraid we had to let her go. Well young man….' Inspecting a dried-up fish tank in the waiting room, Felix started with a jump. '...this is for you.' The dentist held out a barley sugar lolly. Glorious amber glowed in the air before him, reaching out Felix could almost taste the sweet, mellow, treasure.

Oh, dear me no. We never indulge between meals,' said Mum, dismissing the lolly, in her official role as keeper of the strictly measured treats cupboard. Felix scowled darkly at Ruby; whose little hands had shot out at the sight of the offending sweet. Mumbling a goodbye to Mr Fogg, he resentfully followed Mum and the trolley full of Ruby, out into the afternoon sunlight.

Mr Fogg eyed the little family walking down the drive.

'Not a single cavity,' he hissed, snatching up the lolly off the desk. 'They don't eat sweets. They couldn't possibly do that!' Mr Fogg recklessly hurled the it at the door and the figures that retreated into the

22

afternoon heat. It shattered against the wooden frame, sending topaz shards of sugar all over the worn-out mat.

In the silence, Mr Fogg closed his eyes, blood thumping in his ears. In days gone by the surgery was alive; the air full of the high-pitched whine of drills. Muffled voices, thick with cotton wool. Hushed reassurances, maybe a scream or two? Shimmering before him, the blank faces of hapless mothers, as he patiently explained that their children had to clean their teeth more. Never mind, the finer points of dental flossing. His mind screamed out for a surgery buzzing with fillings, root canals, extractions.

Fool! He bent to collect the glassy debris on the mat, shaking his head in disbelief at his own feeble ploy. Sweets, Arnold Fogg giving out sweets. Where would it end? Closing his hand over the sharp tacky mess, a thought struck him. How had this happened? When was it, that he had noticed the holes stop appearing? Silent drills, the empty rooms, his mind swam a little. He could not remember. In the fading afternoon light, Mr Fogg did not move. He stood before the door; eyes firmly shut.

When he did move, the sweet hit the bin with an empty metallic clatter.

On this day.

Granny emerged from the shadows at dawn. High above the village, she watched long fingers of golden sun stir the birds in the woods. Inching down narrow streets it roused the village, stroking terraced rooftops, before stretching out over the valley towards town.

She was waiting. Rolling a pebble between her palms, Granny stared hungrily at the houses below her. Taking her place on the edge of the tower, she was ready.

'I still can't change your mind?' said a creaky voice, from just by her elbow.

'Nope,' replied Granny.

'Well then…' said the voice, leafing through the newspaper laid out before it.

'Well, what?' asked Granny.

'What?' queried the voice, rifling through a few more pages. Annoyed, Granny rolled on her side to look at him. 'Well then, get on with it. We haven't got all day,' he said, pointing at the paper. 'The crossword is waiting.'

'You're trying to distract me, aren't you?'

'Yes, is it working?'

Below them, letters arrived on mats. Cold milk was clinked onto shady steps, and the bakery lifted its blinds to the morning sun. From high above, Granny saw the car she was waiting for begin the winding journey towards the village. She twitched the pebble between her fingers. A front door slammed shut below, dragging her attention back to the village.

'Aha! There he is.' Granny had spotted Archie Burton, serial vandal, and now the focus of Granny's, special attention. Archie marched down the streets, whacking the heads off flowers as he passed the well-tended window boxes and gardens of SnickerFord village. She tapped the pebble impatiently, as he kicked over a line of wheelie bins at the end of an alleyway.

Archie reached the bus stop, just as the car passed by. It slowed, stopping to park outside the bakery. Sergeant Blomley, of the SnickerFord Police, clambered out of his patrol car and into the shop in order to buy his breakfast. After a wary look around, Archie dug into his school bag. Finding a big marker pen, he began to write across the timetable displayed in a panel on the glass bus shelter.

'Now!' she hissed, launching the pebble into the air.

The bakery door gave a jingle and the Sergeant stepped back into the morning light. Clutching his breakfast in a paper bag, he strolled back to the car without a care. Blomley's only thought was to find a shady spot until lunch time, and hope that there would be some apple turnovers left when he returned.

Archie fumbled dropping his pen. The flying pebble gathered velocity. Chasing the pen into the gutter, Archie rummaged in the dust, losing the lid as well. The tiny stone bore down on the bus stop, Granny held her breath.

With a cry, Archie grabbed the pen, rising triumphantly clutching it in his dirty fingers. Spotting the lid, he rose for a second time, when something fast whisked passed his ear. Archie frowned for a moment, and the bus shelter behind him exploded with a resounding, Boom!

Sergeant Blomley landed on his breakfast, as he dived to the pavement in shock. Birds rose from the woods in a disapproving cloud. Archie, gaped at the millions of tiny glass chunks littering the pavement, the explosion still ringing in his ears. Chuckling horribly, Granny clapped her hands in delight as echoes of her attack faded down the valley. Down below, a bewildered Archie flung away the pen and let out a well-practised sob.

'You know, you really need to get out more,' said Colin sagely. He peered down at the drama below.

'Oh, shut up.' With a bony finger, she pinged a fine silvery thread that almost knocked him off his web.

At the edge of SnickerFord village, before the road disappeared into the hills, stood a huge chimney. Looming above the countryside it had been there forever. No one could remember how long exactly, because the date on its yellow sandstone plaque had worn away. Neat, ancient, and overlooked. A relic of times gone by when big chimneys stood for something, mostly large quantities of smoke and a whole team of chimney sweeps.

These days, SnickerFord had a reputation for greater things than the chimney. Prize-winning chrysanthemums, grown by the fiercely competitive village council, were the talk of the county. The pure clear waters of the ford, and wonderful periodontal health of the community, had helped make SnickerFord an enviable village on any map.

As for the chimney, only the local children ever approached it. Everyone had tried to get in through the wooden door at the bottom, but it never opened. Losing interest, the children would move on and forget. For the villagers, it was just a tower. However, for Granny Green Teeth it was home. Hiccupping gleefully, she wiped a tear from her eye, as Sergeant Blomley led Archie away from a cluster of angry villagers.

*

That evening, Felix Van Doore looked at his own face in the mirror. It was the last day of school term, and somehow, the bus stop had exploded. He had walked with his friends the two miles to school, enjoying the sunshine and giddy with anticipation at the long summer holiday. Admiring a small patch of sunburn on his nose, Felix approved of the extra freckles. Ruby did not have those.

Across the landing happy squeals of laughter erupted from Ruby's room. Toothpaste squeezed neatly on his brush; Felix gently pushed the bathroom door open to listen. Dad's voice caused more shrieks of laughter, ones that threatened to shatter the mirror. Felix slammed the door shut impatiently. What a traitor Dad was! Felix dug around his teeth resentfully, each one receiving the full force of his anger. A sudden rap on the door caused him to pause. 'Make sure you clean your teeth properly Felix, or…'

'Yes! I know,' he shouted through a mouthful of foam.

'Or Granny Green Teeth…'

'Will come and make them green, I know!' he roared, louder this time. Rinsing his mouth, he rolled his eyes wishing they would stop treating him like a baby.

More squeals echoed about the house. Felix was just wiping his face, when Dad rushed through the door with a potty. 'Argh!' Felix yelled and shot out of the bathroom. Nowhere was safe. He was about to mouth something he had once overheard on the school bus, when mum appeared.

'Ready for bed then?' she asked. Almost leaping out of his slippers with guilt, Felix nodded. Her arms full of Ruby stuff, she grinned happily. Felix hugged her tightly, and she dropped the pile of multi-coloured frilliness to hug him back. 'Well done you. Now jump in and I will be through in a minute.'

Leaving Mum to pick up the nightmare outfits, Felix shuffled off feeling a little bit shameful. Apart from the noise, the smell, and the horrendous pink clothing that seemed to multiply whenever Mum washed it, not much had changed. Mum had always read with him. Dad always turned out his light. Mum still made his favourite biscuits, and they both tried to help him with his homework. He bounded onto his bed, so it was no big deal. However, Felix sat up eyes narrowed, one sticky paw on his stuff and he would persuade Dad to exchange her, preferably for a puppy.

*

Across town, Ralph Fogg's evening had been more eventful, but definitely not as enjoyable. He was staying at his grandparents, because mother had taken his grandma to a concert. Ralph was not allowed to stay home alone. Despite being fourteen, and in his opinion, quite capable of playing on his computer until she returned.

Alone with his grandfather, things were pleasant enough, the old man had let him bring his gaming stuff, and they had ordered take away. Where it all went wrong, was when his grandfather decided Ralph was due a check up on his teeth. Never the most conscientious flosser, Ralph was horrified when his grandfather insisted that he needed a tooth removing.

Eventually, cash had changed hands. Hardly content, but a hundred pounds richer, Ralph was now sleeping. The swish of a muslin curtain punctuated the regular snore from the bed. His swollen face, lit by moonlight, was flushed against the white cotton pillows.

Outside the open window, ivy bearded the front of the house. It was here a sudden rustle broke the gentle swish and snore. Seconds ticked by, deep in the shadows of Ralph's room someone breathed deeply. A low hum vibrated through the dark and suddenly a figure stepped onto the windowsill. Twelve inches tall, moonlight glowed on slick red material encasing a tidy frame. With a stealthy glance into the gardens, the intruder was through the open window and onto the bed in a moment.

Ralph rolled over with a grunt. Skilfully riding the wave Ralph had caused in the bedclothes, the tiny caller unhooked a utility bag. Edging nearer the boy's head, a gloved hand emerged carefully from one of the pockets. The figure blew gently; silver dust showered Ralph's face in glittering sparks. He sighed, and for the first time that day a smile touched his arrogant face.

Poppy the tooth fairy, pulled back her hood, long red hair flopped down in a neat plait. With a grin, she slung her bag on the bedside table. Striding to the corner of Ralph's pillow she quickly disappeared beneath it. Tooth first, she struggled free dusting a feather from her hair,

'Night off, I'll give her, night off,' said Poppy. With a grimace, she dropped the tooth on the bedside table, perching gratefully on the edge. It was a warm night, and she stretched the neck of her suit to allow a little air in. 'You're a bit old for this game my lad,' she said, noting the tell-tale puffiness of Ralph's cheeks.

A blissful snore erupted from the bed and she giggled. What did it matter; she was already Tooth Fairy of the Year. She shrugged; at least he had not swallowed it. The last couple of weeks had been tough ones for Poppy. She had used her retrieval equipment more than once. No, tonight the snorkel could remain safely in the bag.

With a jaunty swing of her boot-clad feet, she leapt up on the table to reach for the money. It was then she sensed it. Something heavy, thunderstorms felt like this. She stopped; the air around her boomed with silence. Poppy raised her eyes to the child in the bed, ripples distorted the face sleeping before her. The money cut into her palms where she gripped it, her knees shook dreadfully. A dark shadow loomed behind the fairy's trembling form, and then a huge palm descended slowly over her. All her senses fled in terror, dropping the money, she leapt in a panic.

The dull clunks, as Poppy bashed against the sides of the glass jar that trapped her, did not wake Ralph's blissful slumber. With a final thump, she landed dazed upon the table, rolling into her wings. From above, massive grey eyes bore down. Poppy could not scream. Frozen, she watched in horror as a huge finger tapped against the thick glass. The noise shivered through the air, flooding her ears, knocking the strength from her limbs. Giant white teeth appeared, the enormous face before her split into a grin. Hot breath clouded the glass. She closed her eyes tightly, tears oozing onto her white cheeks. Poppy never heard the hissing, and the world went black.

Later.

The summer holidays were almost over. As usual, Granny had resentfully watched children free to play in the woods, ride their bikes, and try the door at the bottom of the tower. Sitting on the edge, she dangled her boots, disappointed that none of this summer's adventures had included the drama of the fire brigade. Gone were the days when summer was a riot. The tinkling of cheap tin bells interrupted her sulk.

'About time too,' she said. Granny heaved on a shimmering cord attached to the bells. Grumbling loudly as she pulled, rays of afternoon sunshine flashed off her long nose. Finally, Colin appeared, riding a wire supermarket basket.

'Ahoy there!' he shouted, waving several legs, one held a hat made from folded newspaper. Popping it back onto his torso at a jaunty angle, he did a twirl for Granny's benefit. 'I'm back, and what a time I've had.'

'Lovely, well you certainly took your time about it. And who have we come dressed as, Admiral Arachnid? Dress like a sailor day is Wednesday. You look ridiculous!' Granny stomped off round the edge of the tower. Colin sighed; he knew that look. The pursed hairy lips, the dangerous frown, he had left her alone for too long.

'Someone seems a little snippy this afternoon. I wonder who that could be? Is it me? No, I don't believe it is.' Supremely unconcerned, Colin's voice droned on. 'I'll just read this article on Origami….'

'Oh, for goodness sake,' she smiled in spite of herself. Flouncing mostly out of habit, she sat crossed legged in front of him. 'Alright, where have you been?'

'Well,' teased Colin, circling a hairy leg provocatively. 'Sure, you want to know?' Granny raised an eyebrow so high that it disappeared into her scrubby fringe. 'Okay then, Mrs Boardman has really got stuck into the re-cycling. Now, I know you thought it was something to do with using old bikes and stuff, but no! Look here.' A dizzying array of newspapers, magazine articles, and quiz books flashed before her eyes. 'That one is a new type of number puzzle, we have loads of those. Mrs Boardman is not good with numbers; they are not her thing. Oh, and there are a few, beauty tips, in that one.' Colin noticed Granny's frown and hurriedly buried the article away for future reference. 'Sharon and Darren next door, have chucked away loads of books to make room for something called a mode –em ….' Hairy legs waved in a mystical fashion.

'A what?' Granny frowned. 'What is it?'

'I don't know. I think it's for fish, I am assured it's the very thing… for all your streaming needs,' said

Colin. Granny watched him as he dragged out more clippings and chatted on about his day.

Colin was a good friend indeed. Hatched in Mrs Boardman's garden, right next door to the tower, he had always lived in its shadow. Whilst his brothers and sisters had spread throughout the village, Colin had been content to stay and live with his mother in Mrs Boardman's cosy terrace.

Mrs Boardman was a nice woman. She had never disapproved of them living in doors, and she was a big fan of crosswords and puzzles. Colin had often dangled from the safety of the light fitting in the living room, watching quiz shows on the television. Her love of cats was the only thing that disturbed Colins peace.

Eventually, Colin had grown tired of the life or death dash across the carpets and rescuing his mother from inside the vacuum cleaner. After Mother was tragically squashed, during a misunderstanding with a houseguest, and vacuumed away for the last time, Colin had left Mrs Boardman's, climbing the tower for a different view on things.

Life on the Tower had turned out to be very different, but at least Granny had never stamped on him. Whilst he always attended quiz night at the local pub, a key member of the Hairy Eights, Colin was never happier than up here with Granny.

'So, then he said he would try it, 'said Colin.

'Try what?' Granny shook herself.

'Kevin, he said...'

'Have you been drinking?' Granny's nose zoomed down, a breath away from his pincers.

'I have not,' he replied indignantly. With one long leg, he delicately pushed Granny's nose away. Underlined by a sprinkling of shadowy hairs, it was not something to view close up through numerous eyes. 'Yes, I have been to the pub. Kevin said he would web up the families toothbrushes. I have told you how anti-spider, she is. Well, if he does it just before bedtime, with some really grubby ones from behind the bar, she will never let the family use them. They go to bed. You are out, and she will have a lot more than Kevin to worry about. So, what do you think?'

Granny opened her mouth. What could she say? Colin was forever coming up with plans to get her out, yet those plans had always come to nothing. Granny had not been out since they buried old Mr Eady, her last customer. Even before that, it had all been a bit of a chore. For years, she crept in at the window, turning the dentures on his bedside table green. He had never noticed, and the nurse rinsed them clean in the morning. It never lived up to the old days, when doing the teeth was only part of the fun.

Watching them bury Mr Eady in the tiny churchyard below, the whole village gathering in rows of black along the streets, she knew he was the last. The curse was complete, she had trapped herself here.

Colin coughed, a few eyes blinked at her, others glowed with impatience. 'Great,' said Granny nodding. 'That is a great plan. We will just have to watch for the signs.' Scampering excitedly over her threadbare skirts, Colin shot up the dirty jacket to her shoulder.

'We'll watch together,' he said. She turned her face to the village below, where lights had begun to appear in the sweltering dusk. Colin caught a shimmer of damp at the corner of her eye. Softly, his creaky voice rustled in her ear. 'Who knows, after all this time, you might just explode?' Her shriek of laughter echoed out across the rosy coloured evening sky and off into the valley.

Below, a hand turning the key in the bakery door, stopped with a shiver.

'I hate that owl!'

*

Down the twisty road from the village, summer heat had baked the flowerbeds in Snickering Civic centre. Only the town cats patrolled the sweltering streets. Poised on the wall of the memorial gardens, a large, grey tomcat surveyed the undergrowth intently.

Nothing moved amongst the roots, the air was too still for a rodent's peace of mind.

His sharp eyes caught a flicker across the square. A shadowy outline darted into view. Watching as a spindly form leapt from lamppost to lamppost, amazement pinned the cat to its perch. The dark figure lurched and swayed in a crude notion of stealth.

The scuffling of big feet broke the spell, and the cat leapt away in disgust, leaving the prowler gasping through a woollen balaclava in shock. With no more lampposts to hide behind, the gangly shadow made a leap for cover under the window of the travel agents.

Above the grocers shop a head appeared. A tabby cat rested on the slates, idly watching the human squirm along the pavement. Under the front of the chemists, and past the coloured displays in the charity shop window, before finally arriving on the steps of the local newspaper office.

Silver glittered in the streetlights as the shadowy form unrolled a pouch. Shaking hands selected and rejected slim flashy instruments, trying each in the simple lock of the front door. The smell of human panic drifted up to the tabby. With a long stretch, and a flick of her tail she bounded away over the rooftops, abandoning the figure muttering in the dusk.

The frantic rattling of the lock ceased, as the prowler noticed that a window had been left open.

Moments later, large feet disappeared through the space that had not admitted a draft all day. Rattling and thumping, the intruder cast aside the window blinds, spooking a scrawny kitten hunting in a nearby alley. Silence settled into the shadows of Snickering High Street. Warily, two eyes emerged, peaking around the various articles and adverts stuck to the window, checking the deserted streets. Slowly, the eyes disappeared, and the figure melted into the shadows of the wordsmiths.

*

The next morning, Sergeant Blomley puffed with effort. Wobbling dangerously, he negotiated the high street on his police issue mountain bike. The town bustled with early morning shoppers, crowding the marketplace, stepping out with very little warning. An alarm wailed into the air, cutting its own path through the rows of market stalls. Trying to steady his bike, after a near miss with yet another tartan shopping trolley, Blomley glanced down the side road to the source of the noise.

Out on the steps of the newspaper offices, stood Mrs Sweet, the ancient receptionist. Fingers in her ears, she tapped her toe impatiently against the racket. With a hollow squeal, Blomley hit the brakes. Dragging the cycle to the corner, he popped his head around curiously. Sergeant Blomley dared not go any further. It did not do to catch Mrs Sweet's attention.

In charge of the birthday club, Mrs Sweet had plenty of gap- toothed, freckle faced photographs in her archives to control of the locals. Nobody wanted to appear in the 'Look who's Forty' section, to be reminded of their braces, or the fringe you mum had sworn was straight.

Officer Roberts bustled up the steps note pad at the ready, just as the alarm stopped abruptly. 'Very messy, luckily they had left my desk alone,' said Mrs Sweet. Her definite tones reached Blomley.

'And, nothing was stolen?'

'No Officer Roberts, nothing at all. Now, if you will excuse me, I still have some important competition winners to type up, in spite of the mess in there.' Blomley heard the tapping of Mrs Sweet's heels as she retreated into the offices. Feeling safer, he climbed back onto his cycle and silently wheeled into the street.

'Nice bike Sarge!'

Sergeant Blomley grunted, cheeks flaming under his helmet, he set off up the long road to SnickerFord. Blomley did not have time to bother about cheeky young officers. The councillors in SnickerFord village, they could be a difficult lot, and this recent wave of vandalism had him worried. Archie Burton, now he was trouble. The Snickering Guardian could sort itself out.

On Felix's birthday.

A car pulled into the long queue waiting to leave the muddy field. Warm and cosy inside, the wipers slid fat drops of greasy autumn rain to the sides of the windscreen. Dad looked down at Felix in the passenger seat.

'Good birthday?' asked Dad.

'Great birthday,' replied Felix, his freckled face split with a wide smile.

'Which was your favourite part of the show, you two?' called Dad to the boys in the back seat.

'The clowns!' Will yelled, his head appeared between the seats in a flash, 'How cool was that? The water, those cream pies, and covering Ralph Fogg in all that foam. Ha! Did you see him cry?'

'Yeah, like a baby,' Jamie bounced excitedly in his seat.

Felix turned to face them. 'I bet you, he gets someone at school the first time we have custard,' he declared. Secretly, Felix thought riding in the front of the car with Dad was the very best part of his birthday, but he kept that to himself.

It had been fantastic; Will and Jamie had stayed over, all weekend. None of them had slept until two in the morning. Even then, they had only gone to sleep because Mum threatened to join them if they didn't. Felix had hushed them and snuggled down, blissfully happy knowing that Ruby would not be waking anyone. No, because she was packed off to Nana Van Doore's for the whole time.

Pizza, pillow fights, presents, and finally, a trip to the circus. All, Ruby free joy. Contentedly, Felix watched the traffic move about the muddy car park, his father happily chatting to the boys. Until Jamie got bored.

'Mr Van Doore?' interrupted Jamie.

'Yes, Jamie?' replied Dad.

'Why did you go outside, when that lady on the trapeze span by her teeth?'

'Actually, I'm not too comfortable with teeth stuff,' said Dad, watching for his turn to move the car forward. Felix twisted between the seats to see his friends.

'Dad's got a bit of tooth thing, don't you Dad?'

'Mm,' said Dad absently. Closing his eyes briefly, Dad tried to forget the sparkly, tooth-abusing spectacle that had launched him out of his seat. Shoving his way out, back into the entrance tent for more popcorn, he had run straight into the arms of Mr Fogg, the dentist.

Mr Fogg had been standing in the foyer with young Ralph, who was complaining loudly about his eyes. They were pleasant enough, and Mr Fogg certainly was brown for his holiday abroad. Then, Mrs Fogg had swaggered over in her fur coat boasting about how clever, 'Ralphie,' had been to win the trip in the local newspaper. When she started to complain about how hot it had been in Australia, Dad decided he would take his chances with the trapeze artist, fleeing back to his seat, relieved to see jugglers flinging ping-pong balls about.

'Why?' asked Jamie.

'Why, what?' Dad emerged from his nightmare.

'Don't you like stuff to do with teeth?'

'It's a long story.'

'I don't think we are going anywhere soon, Mr Van Doore,' said Will, pointing between the seats to the long line of traffic before them.

'I had a nasty experience, alright. Shall we just leave it there?' Dad sagged in his seat.

'Come on Dad, it can't be that bad,' said Felix.

'Please!' The three of them pleaded together.

Dad gave in, with a heavy sigh. 'When I was six, I lost all my teeth in the night. Okay?' They sat stunned for a moment, before Felix burst out laughing.

'What, like, all of them?' said Jamie. Dad nodded into the rear-view mirror.

'That can happen?' asked Will gravely. Dad's eyes rested on the face in the mirror, he nodded slowly, Will's eyes opened wide in the dark interior of the car.

'No way,' giggled Felix. 'How could that happen?'

'I don't know, but it did.' Dad shook his head. 'Your Uncle Stefan said, it was because I had slept with my head under the pillow.'

'This is a joke, right. You never really lost your teeth?' Will was pale now, eyes like saucers.

'You asked me,' Dad replied.

'I sleep like that all the time; how could that happen?'

'I don't think anyone ever came up with a reason,' said Dad, squirming at the memory. 'Stefan lost a tooth, and your Nan put it under his pillow for the tooth fairy. In the morning, he had got his money, and I had no teeth.' Will gasped, the others snorted with laughter. 'I'm serious! Your Nan was furious, she thought Stefan had played a trick, that he'd coloured them in or something. It was bad at the dentist as well. She got hysterical when Mr Fogg told her he had never seen anything like it. She whacked him with her handbag. Anyway, they grew back quickly after that.'

'So, why don't you like teeth, if they grew back?' asked Jamie, ignoring the furious look he got from Will.

'Have you ever woken up with no teeth Jamie? It is an experience you never forget.'

'Yeah, like Nana Van Doore in a temper,' Felix giggled.

'I heard that!' Dad reproached. 'Now, if you don't mind, I'd rather forget about it, eh Will?' Will nodded, mouth firmly clamped shut. Gratefully Dad switched on the radio, and the traffic crawled forward.

They lost interest in Dad's teeth and started to poke each other with souvenir light sticks bought from the circus. Falling out of the car at the Van Doore house, they clattered inside, to find all of their mothers sipping tea together at the kitchen table.

The clamour of voices, and waving light sticks got louder, until Jamie's mother shouted over the noise, 'Right, it's time to leave. Get your stuff.' Will and Jamie bundled up the stairs to collect their things. Felix grinned at Mum, as happy as he had ever been.

'Happy Birthday Felix,' said Will's mother, rising from the table. 'May I take another peek at that beautiful girl, before we go?' Felix's smile froze, Mum nodded.

'Ruby's back?' asked Felix casually.

Mum ruffled his hair.' About ten minutes ago. I think your Nana wore her out.' They shared a smile. Nan Van Doore was a very early riser. 'She's asleep in the living room.' Felix hugged his Mum hard.

'Thanks, this was my best birthday eve…' began Felix. He was interrupted as Will's mother dashed back in, grabbing a tea towel from the table,

'I think she woke up! It's just a mess, that's all, no damage,' she said with a laugh. Rushing past Felix, his mother arrived at the door, where she too began to giggle.

How did she do it? Felix stood bewildered in the kitchen. Ten minutes, Ruby was only back for ten minutes. Everyone was all over her, and she had managed to make a mess. Then a thought sneaked up on him. The living room was where he had opened his presents. Ruby had made a mess. Felix started to get hot around his knees. One of his presents was a giant-sized bar of delicious milk chocolate, a treat even Mum could not deny him. He shoved roughly into the doorway,

'Felix, don't push please.'

He knew it! Ignoring Mum, he stood rooted to the spot, insides boiling. Red faced, Felix stared at the small dark-haired girl, sat amongst a pile of ripped, shiny, paper. On her face, her hair, the pink cardigan and flowery tights, was his chocolate. The remote control of his brand-new game's console clutched between her brown sticky hands. Slowly, Ruby nibbled the edges, dribbling chocolate over the buttons. The blood rushed to Felix's head.

'No, no, no! 'yelled Felix. Grabbing the slippery remote control, he yanked. Ruby held on, a surprising look of defiance. 'Get off,' he demanded. Ruby pulled back. 'Stop it,' he shouted. 'Stop it, you stupid baby!' Oblivious to the gasps at the door, Felix wrenched, tearing it from her grasp. Slipping through his fingers, the remote control sailed across the room landing somewhere with a smash. The toddler teetered for a second, before she too landed with a thump.

'Felix!' Mum dashed in to scoop Ruby up.

'She ruined it,' he said. 'That was mine and she took it and ruined it.' Ruby started a long slow wail. 'Shut up!'

'Stop it Felix,' said Mum firmly. Oblivious to the chocolate, she tried to soothe Ruby, but the wail soared into a full-blown howl.

'No!' he bellowed back.

'I said, stop this,'

Felix screwed up his face angrily. 'No! I will not, she is stupid. I hate her. This is my stuff and she ruined it all.' He could hardly breathe for yelling. 'You let her get my things. I hate her! She ruined my stuff! I HATE! HER! She ruins everything, I WISH SHE'D NEVER BEEN BORN!'

Mum stood silent, open mouthed with shock. Ruby turned in surprise; forgotten tears left little white tracks in the chocolate on her face. Felix felt tears of frustration trickle down his own cheeks. He swallowed; throat raw from shouting. They are all behind me, he thought, aware of the very loud silence only other people can make.

The doorway was full of people. At the very centre of the tea towels, sleeping bags and crumpled pyjamas, stood Dad. His usually brown face was an odd shade of yellow, as he stepped into the room, the doorway became empty of visitors. Felix's palms flooded with sweat.

'Go to your room,' Dad said quietly.

'But, it's not fair...it's my birthday...,' croaked Felix.

'Room, now.'

'But...,'Felix looked down, eyes burning.

'Go!' roared Dad. The room sprang back into life. Ruby wailed. Mum bounced, hushing the toddlers tears.

'I hate you! 'raged Felix. Rushing out of the room, he sped past his friends in the kitchen. Banging loudly, he dashed up the stairs, thundered down the landing, and slammed his bedroom door shut. Felix flung himself onto his bed. Letting out a sob, he wept selfish, guilty tears as though his heart would break.

*

'Will you stop that tapping?' Above the village, Granny was having her own problems. Across the centre of the tower, hung a hammock. Finely worked from web silk, anchored from the landing to the staircase opposite, it swung to and fro supporting Granny over the cavernous drop. With a lumpy brown scarf wrapped about her head and under her chin, she struggled as she twisted the multi-coloured cube in her hands

Closer to them, the weather had rumbled around for a while, echoing annoyingly back off the hills. Clouds gathered above the tower, the colour of dirty dishwater. A sudden crack of lightening illuminated Colin. Wearing seven little tinfoil tap shoes, brandishing a pink cocktail umbrella, his feet tapped in a complicated flourish on the smooth sandstone landing,

'No,' said Colin. 'This is the hard bit.' With a swirl, the umbrella span artfully under a leg kicked high. 'I must practice, or I won't be ready for Family Talent Night!' A syncopated clatter, and hairy legs flew in all directions. She grimaced twiddling the brightly coloured puzzle,

'Yes, but does it have to be now, just when I want to do this, this... What is it?'

'A rude, brick, cube,' gasped Colin.

'Well, I would like to concentrate on my rude brick, and you are disturbing me.'

'Oh, come on,' Colin was winding up for the big finish. Tip, tap, tap went the feet. 'You know that Sheila always wins it with her...' Tap- tap- tap. '...Juggling. Well, this year...' Tap, Tap, scrape. '...Is Colin's year!'

'Yes, right! You practise your pathetic tap-dance.' Granny swung faster muttering to herself. Twiddling the cube angrily, she was furious, and of course it had nothing to do with the puzzle in her hands. 'Wow, family talent night, big deal. How does this work? Honestly, a bunch of fools, doing daft things, yeah, great show.'

Colin's feet scraped to a dangerous halt, mid finale.

'Family Talent Night,' she mocked. 'Ooh, terrific. What if these stickers came off?' Unaware of the silence, Granny picked at the stickers on the surface of the block. 'Yeah, let's all practice for our rubbishy

51

show. Oh, this is impossible.' Flinging the cube away in disgust, she glanced at Colin. 'What's wrong with you?' Thunder danced over the tower, filling the silence between Granny and Colin. His arachnid eyes narrowed. Granny lifted her chin.

'How dare you?' he hissed. Granny raised an eyebrow, unsure if she should answer. The elevated brow pushed Colin over the boundary of spider patience. Legendary patience. The type of patience that allows one to keep spinning a web, even when there is a hairy, sad, medieval king, who keeps sobbing into his porridge, watching you. Colin threw down his umbrella. 'Don't ever make fun of my family!' He tore off his shoes, waving one accusingly at her in the hammock. 'Just because your life is boring, and nothing ever happens.'

'Now, hang on a minute,' said Granny.

'No!' yelled Colin. 'My family are fine when you need something, or you are bored. This, as you well know, is the night when we honour our Mother.' Colin kicked open the little match box that stored his tap shoes, flinging them inside. 'Mother squashed in her prime. Crushed, under the giant boot of bigotry.'

'Oh, I thought his name was Françoise.' said Granny. She could not help herself.

'You think our way of remembering Mother is pathetic? Well, you are the pathetic one,' cried Colin

'You, trapped up here, thinking you're so clever. But you are not. She loved variety, Mother did, loved it. But I doubt, you would understand that.' Shocked, Granny blinked. At a loss for a suitable put down, she felt queasy, something prickled inside her, nasty and uncomfortable. 'You madam, are mean, spoilt and selfish.'

'Actually,' exclaimed Granny, rising within the hammock. 'Those are all very good qualities for my job!'

'You don't have a job! What sort of job, requires you to be stuck in a big chimney?' Granny opened her mouth to correct him. 'Yes, all right everybody knows about him, but he's a professional. You, on the other hand, are here, because you are mean!' Colin rose onto his hind legs now. Lightning flashed across the sky. A huge shadow of Colin flickered on the wall, legs waving, his pincers sharp and jagged in the black silhouette cast behind him. 'You don't have anything, but a great, big, nose! If I only had one friend, I would never make them seem stupid. Make what they believe in, seem ridiculous.' Granny's mouth dropped into a surprised O. The hot, prickly, feeling crept up on her again.

'Mm, I know,' she mumbled.

'What?'

'I know. I think, you are probably right,' she studied her dirty nails. Avoiding Colin's angry gaze, she rolled her eyes. 'I may, have gone a bit, too far.'

'Then, apologise,' he said.

'I will not. I've already said you were right,'

'Apologise.'

'What? No, why should I?' said Granny.

'Say, you're sorry.' He demanded.

'You're being unreasonable.'

'Apologise!' Colin's voice deepened, creaking and clicking.

'I...it has a. No!' Granny glared at the irate spider Four little legs sat determinedly on his torso in a formidable pose.

'Apologise!' demanded Colin, stamping a foot.

'N....'

'Do it!'

'Alright!' shouted Granny. She clutched her cloak about her in distress. Colin watched, impassive as she gagged slightly 'Mm.' Her eyes began to water. '...y...'Faced screwed up with effort, her tongue felt too large. She was almost choking. 'N... ssss.' Colin scowled, tapping several feet impatiently. 'Orrreeyy,' retched Granny. Falling into the hammock, she wiped her streaming eyes.

In the silence she caught her breath. 'Ha!' Granny sat up suddenly, a bony finger pointed to where Colin had been. 'You thought I couldn't.' He was suddenly closer, a delicate leg resting on the knotted silk mooring of the hammock. 'Well I can, and I did, so Ha!'

Coldly he nodded. 'Yes, but you were too late,' he said. Colin plucked the silk, it hissed as it slipped apart. Lightening flickered over her shocked face and Granny vanished, straight down.

*

Felix lay huddled on his bed in the darkness. Flashes of lightning occasionally lit up the murky corners of his room. A square of mottled brightness shone in the centre of his carpet. Raindrops ran down the windowpane, animating the glow from streetlights outside. He listened, dry eyed, to the sounds of supper being finished downstairs. Cutlery clinked on plates. Chairs scraped the kitchen floor. He strained to hear the muted conversation between Mum and Dad.

I bet they feel bad, he thought, eating without me. The growling of his empty stomach made him angry. He couldn't even fill up with chocolate, because Ruby was wearing it all. He considered this with fists clenched, then throttled his pillow in frustration. Thunder grumbled outside his window.

Why, had no one been up to give him his lecture? Felix mulled over the various possibilities. Cooing erupted from the adults downstairs, and Felix glared at his carpet. She had probably eaten something green. Despite his best efforts, and some unpleasant side effects, no one seemed to notice when he ate his greens. Dragging his pillow over his ears to block out the noise, Felix pondered on which cunning plan they might use tonight to make him sorry. The naughty step, a time out, possibly grounding him.

Felix leapt up anxiously. What if they had phoned for Nana Van Doore? Felix was always mindful around his Nana. At almost six-foot-tall, Bertha Van Doore commanded a great deal of respect in SnickerFord. She owned the successful garden centre where Dad worked. Overlooking the village, at the top of the hill, it was once the site of her father's farm. A big name in the village, Bertha had no time for Felix's petty jealousy of Ruby. They had discussed it only once. Sat on her knee, steering the giant tractor around the garden centre, Felix had brought up the subject of Ruby. Nana Van Doore had said, 'She's your sister, and you'll be content.'

Mum would never do that to him, decided Felix. She had been unhappy, when Nana had spoken out before. Just after she was born, Felix had shoved Ruby under a gooseberry bush in the soft fruit section, offering her as a gift to some very amused customers at the garden centre. Red in the face, Mum had pursed her lips to Nana's advice. Mum preferred the naughty step, so Felix could think about what he had done. At the time, all Felix thought about was how unlucky he had been to get caught.

Still suspicious, Felix crawled to the window beside his bed. Squinting down the alleyway behind the house, he could just see that the street beneath the orange streetlight was empty. Nana's ancient van was not there. Lightning seared across the dark sky, the sudden brightness blinding him. He leapt from the bed as thunder shook the walls. The weather was not the only surprise for Felix, when he stopped rubbing his eyes, Dad was standing grim faced in the doorway.

*

The walls streaked past Granny as she fell. Righting herself in the rushing air, she fought down her billowing skirts, covering up the grey patched bloomers that were letting in quite a draft. Hairy little sneak! Thought Granny, grappling with the scarf around her head, it swept away upward. She flipped over again. A slow, grudging smile, tortured the already wind stretched face. In her mind, she saw his bushy spindle of a leg, tapping against the mooring of the hammock.

Soot stained bricks began to blur into one. Opening her arms wide, she felt herself slow in the rushing air. Raindrops kept a steady pace around her. Reaching a finger out, she pushed one, knocking others away, they landed with a splat against the wall.

Even her fascination with the raindrops, could not stop the niggling thoughts of Colin. Admittedly, she may have gone a bit too far, but she was so bored. Bored, bored, bored! Yet she knew, without him, life would be unbearable. He had never been this angry with her before, it was so unlike him to drop someone three hundred feet down a disused chimney. Granny spotted the bottom hurtling toward her. Mind you, she thought with a grimace, you had to give him points for style.

*

'I am so very disappointed Felix.'

Felix squirmed uncomfortably; he could tell from the look on Dad's face this was going to be bad. 'Mum and I worked really hard to make this birthday special

and then, you go and spoil it,' said Dad. Felix looked at
the carpet. 'You know, I really wish we hadn't bothered.
We've always known you resented Ruby, but to be so
cruel to her.'

'She ruined my stuff!' gasped Felix. Dad's face
grew darker at this.

'Ruby is a little girl. She didn't do it on
purpose, but to shove her over…'

'I did not shove her, she held onto the
controls.' Dad's eyes blazed at the interruption. 'She
had covered it in chocolate you know,' said Felix
lamely.

'I know, but that is no excuse,' said Dad. Felix
pressed his lips together angrily; he was beginning to
get hot and bothered again. 'Ruby doesn't know what
she is doing.'

'Oh, that's alright then!' Felix burst out.
'She's just a baby, so it doesn't matter. She gets away
with it.'

'What on earth, Felix, what is wrong with
you?' said Dad. 'You ruined your birthday,
embarrassed your mates, and really upset Mum.' This
catalogue of errors infuriated Felix, burning with
injustice, he leapt to his feet.

'Well, I wouldn't have if SHE hadn't eaten my
CHOCOLATE!' he shrieked. Lightening arched over

the village, flashing into his room. Dad stared at the red-faced child before him. Felix trembled.

'I think you had better get ready for bed,' said Dad gruffly, turning to leave.

'But I haven't had my supper yet,' spluttered Felix.

'No, and this time, you will not be getting any.' Dad closed the door, only just managing not to slam it. Felix stood bereft for a second, aware something had happened, but he was not sure what.

'Dad,' he shouted. Yanking open the door Felix shot through, never noticing it bash against the chest of drawers. Books clattered to the floor. 'Dad!' At the top of the stairs, Dad glowered at him.

'You can bang all the doors you want, but you will go to bed immediately.'

'No, I didn't,' Felix was confused.

'No?' Dad asked.

'I didn't ...' stammered Felix. 'I want to...'

'What you do, or do not want, is no longer important Felix. Get washed, and then get to bed.'

'It's not like that, I ....' Felix was desperate to apologise, but Dad just would not listen.

'Right, now!' Dad insisted. Striding toward the bathroom door, he shoved it open. Felix could not believe this. Dad would not listen, and he wanted to apologise. Above him, Dad's flushed face was terrible to behold.

'I wanted to,' squeaked Felix, as he sped through the door. It slammed neatly shut. 'Say sorry,' he whispered to the panelled door. Drooping, Felix leant his hot forehead against the wood, tears filling his eyes.

'Get washed,' barked Dad, at the silence from the bathroom.

Jamming the plug in the sink with shaking hands, Felix panicked; a jumble of thoughts running through his head. How had that happened? Dad must hate him! Why was he not listening, he always listened before? Where was Mum? Tears slipped down his face, he fumbled with the taps. Ruby had caused this. She was taking over. Water flew everywhere, and Felix knocked the soap dish off the sink with a thud.

'Stop playing for time!'

'I'm not,' groaned Felix to his reflection in the mirror. Water trickled from the damp fringe, down his white freckled cheeks. This never happened before her. She had done something to them, he decided grabbing a towel. Something maybe, hypnotized them. Yeah, that was it!

Rubbing his face hard, Felix tried to gather his thoughts. No, that was a stupid idea. She was just a stinky baby; little girls couldn't do that. Mind you, people did tend to go completely gooey over them. He stopped rubbing, thinking hard. Maybe, they did have powers. Maybe, it was... He shook his head. Don't be an idiot, anyway, they wanted her.

Felix gasped; the room swirled. Unnoticed, the towel crumpled into a soft white puddle about his feet. They had wanted her, because… because. They did not like me anymore! Felix's hands rose to his quivering lips. Cold fingers of dread inched around his heart, digging icy nails in painfully.

'Felix clean your teeth,' called Dad, alerted by the silence in the bathroom. Felix stared at the white panels of the door, knowing Dad was just outside.

'Or what?' sneered the angry voice in his head. *'What do they care?'*

Abruptly, Felix picked up his toothbrush, turning on the tap. Cold water ran over the empty bristles. Rebellion made his heartbeat faster, the daring thrill causing him to tremble. After a while, Felix turned off the tap and placed his toothbrush back into the glass.

After the lights go out...

This is nice, she thought. Hovering a few feet above the brick floor of the tower, Granny floated on her back. With a flump, her cloak arrived. Bobbing on the swell of warm air, Granny focused on the pinprick of light that flashed high above. The magic that controlled the vortex about the tower, had created this hot little down draught, strong enough to break her fall.

Enjoying the warm, Granny let her mind wander, when something rustled near her ear. In a flash, her hand shot out and grabbed it. It rattled. On further examination, it proved to be the matchbox where Colin kept his tap shoes. She smiled, had they been down here, Colin could have practised to his heart's content. Well, she would give it a bit longer and then fetch him. Matchbox griped in her bony hand, she lay back, ignoring the tight feeling in her throat.

A whoosh made her ears twitch, and the old brown scarf poured neatly out of the air onto her face. 'Argh!' she shrieked. With a heavy sigh, her eyes followed the winding staircase that circled the inside the tower. Hundreds, upon hundreds, of steps, each with a stone landing that led right to the very top. She rolled her eyes, an apology, and she had to climb all those stairs.

Swimming wildly to get to the steps, threadbare skirts mushroomed about her; Granny struggled against the warm air that bounced her about. With a grunt, she finally dragged herself to the stone steps. The hard rectangle of cardboard that held Colin's shoes, stuck painfully into her palm. Uncurling her fingers, Granny inspected it. Streaked with dirty pink, one side was almost smooth beneath her fingertip. Pushing the drawer open slowly, a faint tang of sulphur and mould drifted up her nose. The shoes sat lifeless in the corner; dull tin crumpled into shape.

What a fool she was! An unwelcome tang behind her eyes shocked Granny. She was jealous. The other spiders never climbed their chimney and she was too proud to ask. However, Colin might have suggested that they held their talent show up here. Obviously, she would have refused. After two or three days, then of course she would allow it. This was Colin's home as well.

Granny sprang to her feet. Stashing the box in her grubby green jacket, she strode upwards brushing away the rain that must have landed on her face. Stuffing down her feelings, Granny hummed to herself as she stepped upwards.

'If I only had one friend,'

'One friend,'

'One friend!'

Goose pimples rose up on Granny's skin. Did she just hear that? She listened hard. Nothing, thunder made no impact here. Granny pressed her fingers to her lips. Had she said it? She could not have, because; she had other friends. Maybe not 'friends' exactly. Admittedly, the one friendship she did have before had not worked out well.

Her throat closed, she slumped to the steps. Granny hated this. Colin had never made her say the, s' word before, he knew it was too hard for her. But mostly, he had never her made her say it, because she had saved his life.

Colin had arrived on the tower one spring evening, carrying a web bag full of scrap paper. Granny had watched through lazy eyes, as he struggled to drag his things onto the sandstone parapet. Exploring with great excitement, Colin had surveyed his new home making grand plans, before watching the sun go down over SnickerFord, and drifting into an exhausted sleep.

In those days, Granny was far too preoccupied to warn silly spiders about the dawn frost. She had just noticed a sudden downturn in custom, people were really catching on to this teeth cleaning business. Sometimes, she went for weeks without a sniff. Colin forgotten; she was disturbed the next morning by the raucous shriek of a magpie. It was the answering shout, that roused her from her chair.

'Get lost! You'll never take me, you feathery fleabag,'

In her opinion, that was a bit optimistic for a spider faced with a cocky magpie. Expecting the spider to be pecked in an instant, she was impressed by his fighting spirit, and one spectacular move where Colin had poked the bird in the eye with a small sharp stick. Granny had unlaced her boots.

Joined by its mate, the magpie squawked loudly. Colin, two of his legs stuck to the morning frost, had curled into a ball waiting for a razor-sharp beak to deliver the fatal blow. Instead, there was a heavy thudding. The scratching of claws on sandstone, and the birds screamed wildly. In the silence that followed, Colin emerged from between his trembling legs. Before him were two, very grubby, sock clad feet.

'Tonight, make sure you find some cover,' said Granny, but Colin had fainted. She released his frozen legs with her own hot breath, and they had been best friends every day since. With a strangled moan, Granny clutched her chest with a fist, she hated all the fuss and nonsense. It was time to sort this out. Then maybe, just maybe, she would let him persuade her to hold Family Talent night here in their tower.

High above, up the winding stairs, Colin stood alone. The sound of Granny's boots ricocheted up the chimney. His eyes swivelled up to the sky beyond and Colin pondered on the colour of the clouds.

*

Down in the village, the storm had left a fine misty rain behind. Felix drummed his fingers on the mattress. This was a complete waste of time, he decided. Streetlights at the end of the alley, cast an eerie glow into the gloom. Bored, Felix leapt up swishing open his curtains. He squinted up and down the alley. Unable to see much in the dark, he rested his head on the cold glass before him. Out of the corner of his eye, Felix caught a movement in the shadows. He froze, only his hot breath making rapid clouds on the windowpane. Felix's heart pounding in his ears.

Slam!

A face reared up from behind a wheelie bin, and the wild grey beard of Mr Ashton from number forty-two, caught the light. Felix squealed, the shock sending him off the bed with a thump. Downstairs, the living room door opened. The quick blast from the television had him pouncing rapidly back onto his duvet, just in time.

'Alright there?' asked Mum, appearing swiftly at his door. She had not spoken to him since the affair in the living room, the silence hung heavily between them. Felix gave in.

'Yeah,' he said.

'Felix,' she said, venturing further into the room. 'You know it will be fine, don't you?' Felix turned to her gratefully, she sounded so sure. Why had he doubted? Of course, Mum would be on his side. 'We will sort it out,' she continued. 'Then maybe, one day, you and Ruby could be friends.'

Raindrops on hot coals could not have evaporated faster.

'We love you both. You and Ruby are very important to us. She is your sister Felix, and one day, that will mean something to you to,' said Mum, moving to the bed and shifting the fringe from his eyes. Beneath her hand, Felix clung to the icy smile frozen across his face. Was she completely mad?

'Now, let's get you into that bed.' Lifting the covers, Mum helped him under. At the door, she smiled tenderly. 'It will be okay, I promise. Goodnight.'

'Night,' he said through gritted teeth. Unbelievable, he thought angrily pounding his pillow into a lump. Flinging himself down, he prayed something would happen. Anything, just no more Ruby.

*

Granny rounded the final turn in the staircase, 'Colin,' she called. 'I have... got your shoes.' Her legs burned uncomfortably. There was no reply. 'Colin?' Granny roared. 'COLIN! Don't be a prima donna.'

'Don't shout, I'm here,' his voice came from the shadows.

'Phew, well that was fun, don't you think?' she said. 'I got your shoes.' Holding out the matchbox, Granny searched for a glimpse of him.

'Thanks.' There was a brief, awkward, silence. 'Do you remember, we discussed nothing ever happening? You know, here, to you?'

'Hmm, you mean the bit when you told me my life was boring, then you said I had a big nose and you dropped me down the hole? Yes, I remember.'

The cautious spider cough was almost imperceptible. 'Yes. So, anyway,' he said.

'Oh, don't worry about it, I'm fine,' she laughed. Colin stepped out of the darkness. He shimmied toward her, every hair on his body stood up on end. Ruffled up, he resembled a little black pom-pom. Granny, still desperate to make amends and avoid a second apology, gaped at him. 'That is, nice. Fluffing is it part of the outfit?' she stammered.

His eyes rolled upward, following his stare, Granny saw the seething mass. Above the tower, were clouds of a different kind. Her eyes started to glow, blue, full of strange light. Together they watched muted orange gases, swirl within deep grey clouds. Veins of ice blue, static, cracked and sizzled over the surface. Tendrils twisted about the clouds growing brighter, sparking together, strands of wiry light reaching toward the tower.

Colin tore his eyes away for a brief glance at Granny. Her face was contorted in a hideous grin as light played over her coarse features. She leant toward him, poking gently with a lanky finger,

'I think somebody, forgot to clean their teeth!'

'It would seem so,' replied Colin, meeting her magnificently arched eyebrow with a smile.

Unable to control herself any longer, Granny leapt up the remaining stairs with an excited yelp. No wonder Colin was cranky, it seemed so simple to her now. The magic had collected above them, just like the old days, but they had not even noticed. It had been such a long time, so very long.

On the last stone step Granny halted, fists clenched, savouring each moment. The clouds churned brighter; orange turned to gold. She stepped out onto the stone parapet, and the power washed over her. Tugging at clothes, dragging at her hair. Now it was real, she could feel it in her very bones.

'Ha, ha!' Arms flung wide, Granny twirled, wallowing in the force that tortured the clouds. Colin carefully stayed back from the sandstone edge of the tower. Breathlessly, she halted before him. 'Fancy a trip out, Spiky?'

'No, no, you go ahead. Get out there and enjoy yourself,' said Colin generously. The one and only time, she had persuaded Colin to ride out with her, he had proved her quite wrong about spiders being sick. That particular jacket pocket had disintegrated years ago. Happy to watch, he was in no hurry to repeat the experience.

With a throaty cackle, Granny turned back to the light. Static fizzed, long fingers reached toward her. Flickering and spitting, energy pulsed into bright cords around Granny lifting her slowly off the stones. An eye-watering column of light blazed out of the clouds hitting the sandstone edge of the tower. A wooden handle emerged unhurriedly from the stone, which rippled like liquid.

'Yes!' Granny screamed. Fists pumping the air as she was flung high over the centre of the tower, a broomstick hurtled toward her. Deftly she caught it by the handle. They started to spin wildly together in the dazzling white spotlights. They turned until the two lights met. Covering some of his eyes with a fluffy leg, Colin squinted at the spectacle. The air rushed upward from the centre of the chimney with a wail. There was a deep boom, and it was all over. Granny and the broomstick had shrunken, to just the right size for sneaking in at a bedroom window. The clouds above fizzled out to nothing. Colin felt the hair lie down on his torso, as he heard her whoop of joy.

'Yeeha! I had forgotten how unpleasant that was,' she yelled.

'Just be careful out there!' Colin shivered. Hovering before him, Granny was the stuff of nightmares. With a cry, she shot away from the tower.

Pushing the broom upwards, Granny raced through the clouds, until the magic pulled her back. Sailing down toward the earth, they dropped like a stone through damp mist into the valley. Twisting skilfully, she let the broom drift for a second, before it raced forward over the village, giving a happy little buck that never came close to unseating her. 'Me too,' she said, patting the handle.

Casually circling the village, they searched the familiar sights. Steering over the river, she delighted in the roar of the water, so very different from the winds around the chimney. Leaving the river at the weir, she rose to hover above the dark trees of the wood. The sounds of village life drew her in.

A dog barked in someone's yard; the throaty alarm echoed off the cobbled alleyways. Music drifted from the public house, wafting down the main road. Muffled voices droned in houses nearby. In their bedrooms children read, or snored. In the case of two very naughty girls, jumped up and down, throwing socks at one another, until their mother silenced them with a snarl. Granny smiled at the two unrepentant faces, eyes screwed shut in pretend sleep, through a gap in their curtain.

The broom pulled gently; there was the job to do. However, she had a visit to make first.

*

In his bed Felix snored, mouth wide open, fast asleep.

*

Before a simple cross in the tiny village graveyard, she stood silently on the wet grass. 'You aren't the last!' she said. Granny did not like to think too deeply, but something had drawn her here. Alfred Eady, she ran her finger over the brass plaque, he was the oldest and longest of her customers. Her silent little goodbye made, Granny leapt on her broom, ready to find her next victim.

Then, her sharp ears caught the sound of a familiar engine driving up the road from Snickering. The temptation was too much, skimming above the terraced houses, she spotted headlights flashing through the trees. The broom shuddered. 'It won't take a minute, and then we will get on with business,' she explained. The broom swept onward, caught up in Granny's mood.

*

'Aliens on top of the Tower? What a lot of rubbish! 'Sergeant Blomley banged the decrepit heater in his patrol car. He shivered silently, cursing Shuggy Mac Duff. Twenty minutes ago, the Sergeant was at home with a cup of tea and a copy of the Snickering Guardian.

That was before Shuggy had arrived. Thumping on the Sergeant's door, resplendent in his usual tin foil helmet, nightshirt, and wellington boots, the local hermit was raving about lights, aliens and the tower. Shuggy was convinced SnickerFord was about to be invaded, because he had seen it through his telescope.

The Sergeant gripped the icy steering wheel harder. Uniform hastily dragged on over his pyjamas, he was on his way to the village. It was futile, trying to convince Shuggy lightning often hit very tall buildings, so the Sergeant had promised to check the ancient chimney himself that very night.

Reception in the valley was never very good, giving into the static, Blomley flicked off the police radio. As he reached over the steering wheel to clear his view out of the misty windscreen, the headlights struck a shape speeding low in the air.

'Argh!' Blomley cried out, covering his head with his arms. Fast moving, the shape flew over the car with millimetres to spare. Swerving crazily across the road, the Sergeant closed his eyes, as the patrol car slid sideways. It landed in the ditch at the side of the road with a squelchy thud. Lights flashing, the siren started with a half-hearted wail, giving up as the wipers squealed into life.

In the car, Sergeant Blomley sat thoughtfully. It could have been an owl, since it did appear to have a beak. Remembering the sound of little footsteps that had run across the roof, the Sergeant decided it was best not to dwell on it. Fighting with the door, Blomley splashed into the freezing water at the bottom of the ditch It flooded his shoes, seeping uncomfortably between his toes. Slipping and sliding, he scrambled to freedom, flopping onto the grass verge covered in mud. Emptying his shoes, the Sergeant took a last look at the stranded car. Wearily, he set off up the long road for home, absolutely certain no one would believe him.

*

75

Granny sniggered, watching the Sergeant trudge dreadfully into the mist. The broom jolted beneath her. 'You're right, we should get to it,' she said.

Rising high above the tree line, Granny surveyed the landscape. The twinkling lights of the village led to brighter lights in the town. Still higher she went. Bright beads of gold stretched to a city glowing in the distance. Houses, high-rise flats, factories, all the lustrous evidence of humanity laid out before her. Beyond that, shimmering chains disappeared to other towns, other cities.

Now, she would find those dirty teeth. With a deep pull of the evening air, Granny sniffed hard through her enormous nose. The breath of a million mouths, dragged from their slumbering owners, swept by in a minty fresh breeze. Until…. Granny looked toward the village in surprise.

'On my own doorstep.' Shrugging at the irony, she checked the leather saddlebag behind her, a deep emerald blush shone from within the pockets. 'Showtime!' Granny blew with the breeze, soundlessly descending on the village.

Granny Green Teeth.

Sniff, Sniff, Sniff! Snuffle!

Felix's eyes opened, it was warm and dark. He rolled over lazily. What was that noise? Feet padded gently across the landing. A light switch was flicked, someone was checking on Ruby. Seconds later, the footsteps faded and the door to his parents' room closed softly. With a grimace, he flopped back onto his pillow.

Dad was wrong, nothing had happened at all. Felix reached for his watch, he checked his teeth in the shiny metal on the back, they were still white. Closing his eyes, Felix decided Dad was not as cool as he had once seemed. Dragging his duvet over his head with exasperation, Felix tried to get back to sleep.

Sniff! Sniff! Sniff!

Instantly Felix was on his elbows. Through the muffled bedclothes he waited, long seconds, but the silence endured. Eventually, Felix lowered his head convinced he had dreamt the sound. Pulling the cover back up, he snuggled down with a superior sigh. Dad was way off the mark, and in Felix's new revised opinion, a bit of baby.

Sniff!

He froze.

Sniff!

Rigid under the duvet, his eyes searched the room wildly. Slowly, Felix turned, heart pounding. There was a slight movement by the window. He slid silently until his back was against the wall at the end of his bed. A shadow bobbed behind his curtain. *Sniff!* Wriggling, he inched his way down to peek under the hem of his curtain. Whatever it was, he suspected his Dad on a ladder, Felix was going to find out.

*

Outside, Granny was sure she had the right window, only she was staring at the frame. Plastic window frames, surely not. With a grunt of disbelief, she collected some of the emerald green powder from her saddlebag. The broom undulated gently as she guided it to the sill inspecting the window, unsure which way it opened.

Granny shut her eyes for a moment. The good old wooden window, what an entrance she used to make. They sprang open with a mere shake of the fairy dust. It was because of this; Granny did not see the glass coming. *Thunk!* She was swept off her broomstick as Felix flung the window open wide. Against the brick wall, Granny was stunned, her nose crushed against the glass, arms painfully high over her head.

Felix looked tentatively out of the window. The yard below was empty. He gave this a moment's thought, not Dad then.

Granny swallowed painfully, through one eye, she saw the back of the boy's head as he leant out inspecting the yard. Unable to see her broom, she probed carefully with her feet, aware the only thing holding her in place was the windowpane.

Felix held still, catching sight of the movement at his side. The cold air nipped, he trembled slightly, then he saw the broom. Amazed, he watched it bob beneath a tiny boot that cautiously searched the brickwork. The deep brown wooden handle and neatly formed sticks were secured with skilfully woven rope, it carried a small satchel of dark leather.

The broomstick appeared to be deliberately avoiding the foot. He stared, mesmerised by the exhausted leather of the boot. It slowed to a self-conscious halt. Squashed behind the glass, Granny was not at her best, the small crushed face made him wince. An angry blue eyed stared at him defiantly from a very dirty cheek. The nose against the glass was fascinating, 'Wow, you have a really hairy nose!' said Felix. The angry boot flailed at the him.

Granny was furious. She did not have to take insults from a mere child, not when she could kick! Felix moved back so the little foot could not reach. Behind his head, the broom floated upwards, juddering slightly, Granny knew it was laughing. She growled.

'I don't think there's any need for that,' said Felix. He would not move the window if she was going to bite him. Granny glared at the broom shuddering behind Felix's head,

'.... ot oou....'

'What?'

'...ddee .... bwwoom.' With a cramped sigh, Granny unfurled her empty hand and pointed. The broom shot above him and bobbed innocently.

'Sorry, I don't understand,' Felix said. Granny was running out of breath, unable to move, she wriggled her feet as much as she dared. She was obviously in pain, but how should he get her out from there? She would fall if he simply pulled back the window. Grabbing a pillow from his bed, he shot back out to check she was really there.

'Granny Green Teeth, I don't believe it! But you can't fly by yourself,' he said, pulling the pillow out of its case. Granny's squashed cheek developed an angry spot of red on it. 'Actually, I never thought about that, you flying, I mean how would you get in the windows? Unless, you had a ladder or whatever. Okay, just drop in.' said Felix, slipping the pillowcase over her kicking boots.

Felix pulled back the window slightly. Granny glared, her face squeaking against the glass as she slid down the pane. Her free hand gripped the window edge, unwilling to let go. Without warning, the landing light flicked on inside the Van Doore house. Felix hesitated for a second, before risking his fingers and scooping the struggling figure into his pillowcase. He dragged her through the window, closing it quickly as footsteps padded up the landing.

Inside the pillowcase, Granny was able to breathe again. Ramming the green powder hastily into her jacket pocket, she fought against the fabric enclosing her. 'Keep still,' hissed Felix. Granny could feel the heat of the child's breath through the cotton. Hairs on the nape of her neck stood up. The child was scared of something, but it was not her.

Footsteps grew closer. Felix swung about. What should he do? Just by the curtains was a slim space between his bed and the wall. Quickly he jiggled the pillowcase, down into it. Bumping her against the wall in his haste. 'Watch it!' said Granny

'Shush,' he hissed.

Pulling up the duvet, Felix tried to control his breathing. The footsteps arrived at his door. 'Felix?' Receiving no reply, Dad opened the door. Light from the landing spilt across the carpet. Under the covers, Felix's hand tightened on the pillowcase. He kept perfectly still, forcing himself to breathe slowly in spite of his pounding heart. Satisfied, Dad closed the door, his footsteps faded down the passage.

Lying there in the dark of his room, Felix suddenly began to worry. He was holding a pillowcase, full of a nasty looking magical being who wanted to turn his teeth green. The bag twitched in his grasp. He was positive she had tried to kick him and after the growling, he was wary she might bite. This was the second time today things had not turned out the way in which Felix had intended. The bag twitched again, as Granny sought more room. With her knees up near her ears, she was cramped and angry.

'Keep still.' Felix whispered. What was he going to do?

'Let me out!' Granny hissed struggling upwards,

'Just a second...,' Felix murmured. Lifting her out of the gap, he crept to his bedroom door pressing an ear to the wood, straining to hear any sounds. He studied the pillowcase full of Granny, it was getting heavy, he would have to put her down soon. What would happen then?

The read out on his clock said ten thirty. Mum and Dad were usually a sleep by now, obviously not tonight, but Dad would have turned out the landing light on his way back to bed. Felix could risk his bedside light. Creeping to his table, he flicked on a rocket shaped lamp, the muted golden glow made him feel braver.

*

Inside the pillowcase, she was furious, a human had never caught Granny Green Teeth. To be fair, none of them had ever tried before. She had hovered over a few, until the sleeper had awoken aware someone was watching, they had screamed a lot. She'd had a few slippers thrown at her in the past, and once a cat, but no one had ever tried catching her.

Nevertheless, a child trapped had her, and who knew what he was going to do? She knew exactly what she would do, if the sack were on the other being. Frantic, she thought of Colin, how he would deal with this? He would fight. She struggled about, but the cotton was well ironed and slippery, all Granny achieved was to tip herself further down the bag until her feet were at the top.

What else?

Be a, 'people person', Colin had tried to teach her this over the years without much success. With her knees by her ears, Granny gave it a go. 'Err ... hello child, we appear to have ourselves a bit of a misunderstanding here,' she said in a wavy falsetto voice. Wincing she put her hands over her face in embarrassment. 'So, if you would just like to help me out of this, thingy....'

'Pillowcase,'

Granny screwed up her face. 'Yes, pillowcase, thank you, dear boy,' Granny gagged slightly. 'Just, pop the pillowcase down...we can sort this little mess out.' Unable to see anything but shadows and light through the cotton, Granny was beginning to feel seasick from the boy's indecisive swaying.

'And?' he prompted her

'Aaand...I'll get out....and ... we'll have a little chat.... eh?'

'Yeah right, I might be a kid, but I'm not exactly stupid,' said Felix. In the bag, Granny raised an eyebrow.

'Erm.... I'm a little deaf young man. You will have to open the bag so I can hear you.'

'I said, I am not stupid,' he repeated, face close to the pillowcase to make sure she heard. Granny lifted a boot ready to kick at the outline of his nose but thought better of it. Meanwhile, Felix had a problem, she was getting heavy, he rested the bag on his mattress. 'Look, if I let you out, promise not to turn my teeth green.'

'Eh?' Granny was unnerved. She was a terrifying spectre, not someone with whom you could bargain. 'Look kid, I can't not make your teeth green, it's my job.' Under her breath she mouthed, idiot!

'You get paid for it then?' asked Felix.

'No! It's just what I do,' she answered slowly

'Why?'

'What do you mean, why? It just... it... just is!'

'Yes, but why?' asked Felix.

'Because,' she snapped. In the pillowcase, Granny wriggled herself onto her elbows, considering her position. The broom was outside. She had to get out, to get away, and the dust in her pocket was not enough to do his teeth anyway. She blew her nose on her jacket. 'I'll promise not to turn your teeth green, yet,' she said.

'But I don't want you to turn my teeth green, at all,' said Felix.

'SO WHY DIDN'T YOU CLEAN THEM!' snapped Granny furiously. 'For goodness sake! This is not optional. You don't clean, they get green, it's worked for years that has.'

'Shush....' Felix hushed her. 'Do you want my Dad to come back?'

'Has he cleaned his teeth?'

'Yes.'

'Then, no!' She kicked the bag hard. 'Let me out of this pillowcase right now! Do you understand? I am not a toy.' Suddenly Granny stopped struggling, Felix blinked as the pillowcase went still. Granny began to suspect, there was more to this than met the eye.

'Do you want your father to come back?' she asked, voice a velvety blanket of concern. 'Mm? After all, you do appear to have captured quite a famous personality here. Are you sure, you do not need Daddy's help?'

A flush appeared on Felix's cheeks. 'No thanks, I seem to have done well enough on my own,' he said.

Granny banged her head on the mattress in frustration. 'Right! I won't turn your teeth green, let me out,' she said blandly.

Shocked by her sudden compliance, Felix was suspicious. 'Promise?' he asked.

'Yeah.'

'Say, promise.'

'Don't push it!'

Slowly, very slowly, Felix let go of the pillowcase. It thrashed about. Granny struggled to right herself, and then she emerged from within the cream pocket.

*

Standing in a pool of light on his bed, right there in his room, was the oddest-looking thing Felix had ever seen. At almost two-feet tall, in her shabby attire Granny's image was not that of your average magical being. A very grubby green tweed jacket covered an old brown jumper, which concealed a once pink flowery shirt. Tattered grey skirts reached down to the laces of her black leather boots. Felix frowned, thinking that she would do well to check out some of the books Ruby had in her room, full of colourful witches with stripy socks, and pink fairies with crowns. It was almost as if she hadn't tried very hard.

Granny's long pointy nose dominated a small chiselled face, giving her a somewhat foxy look. Dark hair, in disarray from the pillowcase, flopped out of her bun falling roguishly over one eye. She did not look so old, and her hair was not grey, in fact she did not look like any sort of granny Felix knew. With a puff, she blew the hair away and fixed Felix in the full glare of her blue slanting eyes. He smiled self-consciously. 'Err, hi. I'm Felix. 'he said.

'Of course, you are,' Granny said, noting the pink freckled face, auburn hair, and red stripy pyjamas. She twisted her hair back, looking about her. His room was a brightly coloured jumble of dinosaurs and spaceships, books, toys and baked clay models. A door at the far end of the room stood open, revealing shelves stacked with clothes and boxes, above the doorframe hung a large rubber T-Rex head. 'You didn't catch that by yourself,' she murmured.

Felix watched every movement, amazed by the hair that still escaped its bun, her lean profile, the hairy brows, and the huge nose. That was hard to miss, but he could never have imagined she would be so shabby.

'Don't stare,' she said. Granny caught the look her gave her garments.

Felix shrugged off the embarrassment. He had so many things he wanted to ask. 'Where do you come from? I mean, where do you live? How do you even know I didn't clean my teeth?' he asked in a rush.

'Mind your own business,' snapped Granny Striding over his mattress, she picked up a snow globe from the bedside table. 'Nice, yours is it?'

'Yeah, it was a birthday present,' Felix said, but he wasn't going to be put off. 'You make teeth green, how, is it a hard job?'

'You would not believe me if I told you.' Granny laughed lightly. Putting the ornament down, she studied the drawings he had done at school that were now pinned to the wall. Cocking her head, she appreciated the skilled pencil sketch of his family, with one smudgy exception. 'Who's that one, in the woman's arms?'

'Ruby,' sneered Felix.

Facing the wall Granny felt his dislike and smiled to herself. This might not be so bad after all, there had to be a way to turn this to her advantage. If she played this right, it would not be another five years before she got out of the tower. 'So,' she said, tiny fists on her hips. Granny marched to his bedside table. The mattress bobbed underneath them, as if cast adrift on an ocean. Shuffling her bottom on to the edge of the table, Granny asked, 'Felix, why am I here?'

'To make my teeth green,'

'Yes, but you are not really the type of boy to go forgetting to clean your teeth, are you? We have never met before, so I can only assume that this was, how shall I put this? Your way of getting something, a new toy perhaps?' she coaxed.

'No!' Felix coloured in the glow of the lamp. 'I do not need new toys, it's my birthday.'

'Oh, many happy returns,'

'Thank you,' he hesitated. Suddenly Felix felt uncomfortable, he hadn't expected her to start asking him questions. In fact, this didn't feel like something he should be doing at all. Pointing at the window he said, 'You know you can leave anytime. It isn't locked.' However, Granny did not intend to leave just yet.

'That's very nice of you. But I want to help you Felix,' she said.

'What?' he replied acidly, eyes blazing. 'I don't need your help. I may have made a fool of myself, but I don't need some old bag's help. Will and Jamie…'

'Less of the old bag, thank you.'

'Sorry but you're a bit, you know,'

'Scruffy?'

'Mm' he nodded. 'My mates….' Felix suddenly thought of the scene in the living room. Would they still want to be his friends after what they saw? His voice faltered. 'They...'

'What?' Her voice wheedled. 'Come on now, surely it was not that bad?'

'It was,'

'Really?'

'Awful,' he said.

'Why what happened?'

90

'Mind your own business,' he replied. Felix raised an eyebrow and smirked at Granny.

'You are alright, kid,' she laughed, with a grudging smile. Felix felt clever in the glow of her approval, he smiled back. They both started, as the church clock struck eleven, the chimes echoed over the damp village. Felix stifled a yawn. Granny took this as her cue. Walking to the windowsill, she pulled back the curtains. 'I like you Felix, so here is what I am going to do. Next time you don't feel like cleaning those teeth, I'll pop over, and you can let me know how you got on with your little situation.'

'What about my teeth?'

'That's more of a tradition, than anything. Let's just say, part of the service.' She shrugged. 'Anyway, who is to say I haven't? So, what do you think?' she enquired. Suddenly he was too tired to care, Felix simply nodded. 'Do the honours will you?' Granny pointed to the window. Opening it, Felix saw the broom anxiously bob up and down seeking Granny.

'That is amazing!'

'It's a bit cranky sometimes, but we get about. Mind you, all these new windows will take a bit of getting used to....' Granny halted, her arm reaching for the broom. Cursing silently, she could have bitten her own tongue off.

'Don't you get out much?' he asked, as their eyes locked together.

'Not as much as I'd like.' she answered warily.

'Well then,' Felix dropped her gaze. 'Maybe, I 'll be seeing you sometime.'

In the morning.

Dawn broke over SnickerFord with a misty muffled light. For Felix, despite his exhausted farewell, sleep had been fleeting. Watching white featureless clouds through a gap in his curtains, Felix could think of nothing but last night and yesterday. Will and Jamie, what would they make of it all? Should he tell them about Granny? She was real, weird, but real. He could barely believe it himself. A wail from the landing startled him.

Ruby was awake, footsteps swiftly headed for the pink chamber of doom. Felix pulled the covers over his head, closing his eyes with a private smile. He had a secret.

*

On the tower, Granny had sat until dawn furiously rocking back and forth in her chair. Waiting for Colin to get up out of his web, she had eventually fallen into a doze.

'What time did you get in?'

Colin's voice woke Granny with a start. She was cold. A fine mist had enveloped the tower. With a shiver she came to her senses. 'Not late. Where were you, anyway? 'asked Granny.

'In this weather, a sensible person would sleep in the warmth down there,' he declared, perching on the arm of the rocking chair. Colin was wearing a hand knitted boiled egg cover, with modifications. Eggs did not have eight legs. The rainbow-striped affair covered his torso cosily. Mrs Boardman had moved on from competitive knitting to tai chi, and so Colin had liberated it.

'You learned that the hard way, didn't you?' she said, standing on stiff legs and yawning hugely.

'I most certainly did,' Colin chuckled. 'Well, let's have it. Which careless fool got a mouth full of green?'

'Nobody,' she replied moodily. Granny dropped her arms and strode away to the sandstone collar of the tower.

'What! Why, what happened?' Colin hurried after her, only mildly hindered by his outfit. Granny spun, taking deep breaths. 'Whoa, watch it; you nearly had me off there!' Colin squeaked. Her skirts almost swept him over the edge, leaping onto the tatty cloth, he scampered upwards concerned and alarmed. She should have been happier than this. 'What happened?' he demanded, clambering onto her shoulder.

'It's complicated...'

'Hello, complicated? Hmm, well now, what we need is someone who likes a good puzzle, a clear-headed, logical mind. I wonder where we could find one of those, all the way up here.'

'All right, there is no need for sarcasm,' she said. 'Not here, it's too cold.' Granny shivered as a wave of slimy mist coated the back of her neck. 'By the way, what, are you wearing?'

'It's funny you should ask that. Do you like it?'

'No.'

'See, I knew you wouldn't. You're so, stuck in the whole, dated 'shabby chic' combo...'

'Colin!'

'All right, Mrs B just started tai chi, so all the knitting ...' Their voices disappeared into the depths of the chimney.

'Let me get this straight,' said Colin, hanging over the stairs in a complicated knot. 'You think this boy will keep his end of the bargain?'

'I told you,' replied Granny. She floated lazily in the heat. 'There wasn't a bargain, it's just instinct. He will not be able to resist, so why not?'

'Well, for one thing, you're going to have to make his teeth green some time.'

'Ah, but he does not know that,' sniggered Granny.

'That's not fair; you should have told him everything,' he said. Colin frowned down at her.

'Not likely! I would never get out if I went around telling the truth. Honestly, would you stop cleaning your teeth if you knew you had to pay for it...eventually?' She chose the last word with care.

'No, I suppose not.' Colin watched her twirl on the hot bed of air, in the light from the fairy dust that had ended up in Granny's pocket. He had provided some dangly webs which Granny covered in the shimmery powder, giving them twinkly lights to illuminate their dark refuge. It was cosy in an organic, swampy, kind of way. 'There are no rules about this stuff then?' he enquired, gesturing to the glittery webs.

'Nope,' replied Granny. A silence fell over them.

'You haven't broken any rules over his teeth?'

'Not exactly...'

'What would happen if you had?' he asked. Colin was following a trail of doubt to its logical conclusion, absolute certainty that something would go wrong.

'Look Colin,' she snapped. Granny sat up angrily. 'What else could happen? I'm stuck here in this rotten tower.' She twirled on the cushion of hot air. 'I mean, honestly! I cannot leave until some stupid human forgets to clean their teeth. Then, I can only go where the magic takes me. Who could do anything, to make this worse? I'm well and truly cursed. It could not get any worse than this, so stop worrying. Aren't there any magazines I haven't read down here?'

Colin thought long and hard.

'About that curse...'

'COLIN!!!'

In the speckled light, Colin worried silently.

*

'Ha-ha, Blomley crashed his car in the ditch!'

The heavy drawl announced Archie Burton's return to consciousness on the back seat of the school bus. Other children pretended not to hear the notorious vandal, now he was awake. With a grunt at the careful silence from the seats in front, Archie contented himself with squashing his face against the bus window. Sergeant Blomley, supervising the recovery of his patrol car, turned puce from trying to ignore him.

Felix had worse things to worry about than traffic jams or Archie Burton. Yesterday had been like some horrible roller coaster, yet this morning was in some ways was worse. Mum, Dad and Felix had been coolly polite to one another, until Ruby had tipped her porridge over her head and made his parents laugh. Felix had tried a smile just to be civil, which had gone down well. The morning slipped into the usual bleary routine of lunch boxes, shoes, and bags.

Shuffling in his seat, Felix ground his teeth once more at the memory of Mum's fond smile at Ruby, and his stifled conversation with Dad on the way to the bus stop. Felix decided Dad was not getting the apology, and he was not going to find out about Granny Green Teeth either. That will teach them, he decided angrily.

Mechanics struggled to retrieve the patrol car, giving Felix more time to think about Will and Jamie. They had both looked so shocked. Hadn't they ever fallen out with a brother or sister, of course they had. Jamie's sister Amelia was not the type of girl you shoved; he could not see Jamie snatching anything off her. However, Will had four brothers; surely, they fell out with each other over stuff.

Felix's train of thought derailed, as the bus squealed to a stop. The door hissed open to reveal Ralph Fogg. Like everyone else, Felix hurriedly slid down in his seat avoiding Ralph's haughty glare as he strode to the back of the bus. Pupils clambered aboard after him; noisily taking their seats as far from the rear as possible. Felix slid back up to find himself looking into shrewd brown eyes,

'Hello Felix, I hear the circus went with a bang.' Felix blushed as Nathan, Will's eldest brother, ruffled Felix's hair carelessly. Smoothing it down Felix glared at Will, as Nathan moved up the bus.

'I didn't say anything,' said Will, slinging a school bag next to Felix. 'Honest!'

'No problem,' said Felix through gritted teeth.

Out of the window Felix spotted a familiar figure galloping around the corner, shirt out, blazer over one arm, Jamie sprinted for the bus. Panting, he pleaded with the driver to wait whilst Amelia, equally as late, made her way elegantly to the vehicle. Careful to thank the driver, Amelia paused to enquire innocently, 'How is Ruby, Felix? I heard she had a fall.'

'She's alright, thanks.' Felix squirmed madly.

'Sorry, mate. She has such a big mouth,' said Jamie, flopping into the seat behind Felix and Will. Before Felix could reply, a loud thump came from the back. The whole bus turned to see Ralph Fogg emerge from the floor clutching his nose. Amelia casually tossed her braids back over her shoulder smiling at the gaping audience, she sat down.

'Yeah,' agreed Will absently. Turning with a grimace to Felix, 'Not something I'm pointing out though. You're on your own there Jamie.'

That does it, Felix thought. He was not telling these two about Granny, they would gossip for sure, and that would be the last thing he needed. He would be out of his mind to let anyone know he hadn't cleaned his teeth.

The Tooth Fairy.

As the first sprinkle of frost descended over the valley, unwary gardeners looked with dismay at the smattering of silver. On the hill above the village, Bertha Van Doore flicked out the light on her desk. Stepping from the office she breathed in the air deeply, smiling as the sharp edge of autumn filling her lungs. In his cottage, Sergeant Blomley dragged back his curtains suspiciously. Letting out a sigh of relief, he watched as his mother covered her tender stemmed plants with excessive amounts of bubble wrap.

Along Snickering High Street, the frigid sky erupted with the leathery flutter of bats in a frenzied cloud. They could barely make it over the roofs, many bounced off the slates. From behind a chimneystack, a pair of eyes watched them in the twilight.

Bats slammed into a nearby shop sign, dropping to recover jerkily. A particularly small one flapped on wearily by. The eyes vanished and the single lens of a camera replaced them, focusing on a low building on the edge of the town. Lights flashed at the windows, blue and sharp against the darkness.

*

'Tell him, 'Tempus Fugit', he'll know I'm right,' he said breathlessly. Colin scampered up to the top of the stairs with Granny.

'You know, you could tell him yourself,' she said. Granny tried to persuade Colin to meet Felix all the time. 'It's just up that street.' She pointed a long finger at the house where Felix and family lived. 'I wouldn't fly fast, honestly.'

A stray firework exploded over the village in a shimmering purple flower of flames. It was week before the village display, but someone was already having fun. 'Course you wouldn't,' Colin smiled. She would not be able to help herself. Granny was just plain naughty, and Colin knew it.

Things were going well for them all. Colin was getting the benefit of a High School education, Granny was getting out a lot, an awful lot. Colin was thankful Felix did not live in the city, who knew what she could get up to on the way out there?

Felix had a secret and he had told no one. Granny's night-time visits were the highlight of his day. Eager to go to bed, his parents had been surprised, then suspicious. Unable to find anything amiss, the family had settled into a wary truce. His teeth were still very white.

Colin retreated to the top step, as the magic crackled into life. With a hop and skip, he leapt onto Granny's hammock. The flash of white light caught the threads on the web, illuminating a whole pile of books and puzzles, in a blue-white glow. All of these had come from Felix's room, and Colin considered him very generous.

Felix and Granny had clicked in a mutually suspicious way. Then Felix had found out about Colin, and his gifts had melted a tiny part of her icy nature. Although, she had yet to realise that a number of the books she took back were actually Felix's homework. With a boom, Granny imploded to miniature. Preoccupied, Colin waved a few legs in response when she called, 'Later!' as she left.

Colin tittered and assumed it was Felix's influence. She would have pulled out her own tongue, rather than admit that a human was having some effect on her, so Colin never mentioned it. That would ruin everything, and he was not about to have her flopping around complaining again. Not with so many books to read. A sudden whistle and a bang over the village, gave way to the itchy crackle of an exploding rocket.

Contentedly, he flicked on the book light clamped to the hammock. Snuggling down into the pile of books, Colin closed all his eyes, reaching out blindly with an elegant hairy limb. Whatever book was touched first, he would read. Feeling like a wealthy spider, he opened his eyes to see what was there. Clicking with joy Colin saw, Magic Tricks for Beginners. Rubbing a couple of legs together in anticipation, he decided that next family talent night, Colin would provide a few surprises.

A whistle echoed up the chimney, the report from another stray firework quickly died away. Colin awoke with a start. The tower was upside down. Blinking all his eyes, Colin realised he had drifted off to sleep and fallen through the hammock again. Since Felix had sent the book light, Colin had been reading at all hours. Stretching his chilly legs, he decided Granny must be back. About to call out to her, he froze. Something was not right, the words died in his mouth.

'She's not here!' called out a shrill voice. Silently, Colin reeled himself back up to the underside of the hammock.

'I can see that,' clipped tones, sniped from the staircase. 'What is all this, junk, doing here?' Colin pursed his pincers at the insult. Footsteps tapped across the stone landing. 'Where is she?' asked the voice. This one was haughty, Colin decided. 'I was told she had not been out in years.'

'Well, she has not... as far... as I ...know.'

Pouncing like a cat, the haughty one questioned, 'As far as you know, why are you not sure?' Colin tingled all over, there was something familiar about the dissecting tone in that voice. Unable to place it; he tightened himself up, listening carefully.

'Well, actually, I think you will find she is a little old for an official visit from the tooth fairy.' Colin almost dropped from the hammock. A brooding silence made him shift nervously. He winced with foreboding, at the coolly detached response.

'You were charged with observing her.'

'It's been twenty years, or more! Do you know how many babies were born? I mean, there was a new housing estate built at the edge of the village, I had loads more work and it…'

'I am not interested in your workload.' Feet marched across the landing above the hammock.

'Look, okay, I used to check with the birds, they would give me regular reports, then about five years ago they stopped coming here.' Colin almost squealed, he clapped a couple of legs across his pincers. 'They wouldn't do it anymore.'

'Why?'

'I don't really know. She threw her boots or something. Nobody flies over here. She's too…well, you know...'

'No.'

'She is... you just have to go around. She's quite mad you know!'

'Nevertheless, her presence is required.'

'Oh.'

'And, she is not here.' That voice could easily have frozen lava. Colin was astounded, the tooth fairy had plans for Granny, which did not make sense. Maybe it had something to do with the boy? Straining to hear, Colin was surprised, the hammock started to swing. Someone was going through his things. Frightened to move, Colin held on tightly. A voice sounded above him, 'What is all this stuff?' The hammock wobbled. 'We have to find her and fast.'

'How are we going to do that? She could be anywhere!' The desperate tone suggested one of them was less than happy about finding Granny.

'Ariel recon, now do stop trembling.'

'Okay,' peeled the hysterical little voice. 'Can we go now?' Colin sniggered; the poor thing was terrified. Granny would be pleased.

'Stop, what was that?' In the tense silence, Colin cringed. 'It's nothing, maybe wind,' the voice decided. 'I'm sorry, are you crying there?'

'No! I've...got something in my eyes.'

'Here.' The tone softened, there was a zippy sound and a rustle. 'Get a grip of yourself.'

'It is just, so, so…. awful. What are we going to do?' she sniffed.

'We search. We catch her and we take her to him. Simple.' There was a sniff, a twang and a flutter, then Colin was alone. The words rang through his brain, *'We catch her.'* Colin shuddered in horror. He would be alone, all alone without Granny. He clicked his pincers together in fear. This had something to do with teeth, he just knew it.

Striking upwards into the papers and books, Colin shoved his way through. Dashing across the hammock, he made for the stairs. Out in the dark, on the icy sandstone parapet Colin rushed about at a gallop. What should he do? He had no idea how long he had slept, or when she would be back. What was he to do? She had to know, he had to tell her. Running to the pulley and basket, he jigged from one foot to another, keeping his legs from freezing to the stone.

'Keep moving, keep moving,' he whispered to himself. They were going to catch her. Trying to focus on the street she had pointed out, he could see lights in the dark, but they all looked the same. He could only make out the public house. Kevin, he knew everyone who knew someone, he could help.

A moment of doubt, made Colin cringe, what if she came back and he was not here to warn her? But then again, they were not looking for her here. Granny was out there, and she may never come back.

Decisively, Colin leapt. Slinging a thread at the pulley, he launched himself from the top of the tower,

'Ooh no, no, no, no! Waaaaaaaaaaah…' Colin did not normally descend the chimney at more than a crawl.

*

Three tiny heads spied on Felix's window from a rooftop across the alleyway.

'This is the place?'

'Absolutely,'

'Oh dear!'

Covering their faces, the fairies wore hoods with great glass lenses that reflected streetlights and fireworks as they watched the house intently.

'You are sure?' Gloved fingers tapped the slates.

'Yes, take a closer look.' The lenses in their hoods clicked as they refocused. 'Use the filter, you can see the broom, she is in there alright.'

'Oh, dear!'

'Let's get in there, we don't have much time.'

'Oh dear!' the sob rang out again.

'What!'

'That's not right,'

'She has to be, there is no trace anywhere else,' said one of them reasonably. 'I don't see why the broom would be here alone.'

'That is not what I meant.' A note pad appeared. 'If I'm right...'

'If?'

The notepad continued to rustle. From the main road, a string of bangers exploded into a cloud of smoky noise. 'It's the Van Doore house,' said the voice faintly.

One of them let out a low whistle. 'She's got some nerve,' they said.

'Interesting,' a voice decided firmly. 'Primrose, you stay here. Bell, you, and I will go in. Let's take it slow, see what she is up to first.'

'Err,'

'What now?'

'I have an appointment. Sorry, you know how it is,' said Primrose.

Three tiny figures stood up on the ridge tiles, with a flutter they leapt. Gratefully, Primrose headed off towards town.

*

They giggled in hushed tones. Slouching in pillows on his bedroom floor, Felix and Granny played Scrabble in the light from the bedside table. They made a cosy sight, only slightly marred by the smell of Granny's bootless feet.

'Right,' he mumbled through a face full of crumbs. 'Your go.'

'Can't,' Granny replied. 'I've run out of letters. Let's play the donkey thing, it is so funny.' She wrinkled up her long nose in amusement. Felix shook his head, handing her the bag of letters.

'No way, you laugh too much. Dad would come in for sure,' he said. Felix wished, not for the first time, that Granny could meet Will and Jamie, but he knew they would not be able to keep it a secret. Mum and Dad would be furious if they found out about Granny's nocturnal visits. And not just, 'think about what you've done', angry either.

Granny was happy. She would rather be out tormenting the world, but it was dangerous. Dodging stray fireworks before bonfire night was becoming a chore. Apart from the tower, where she and Colin had the best view in the world, Felix's room was the safest place to be.

Granny rather liked the boy. He was nowhere near as much fun as Colin, but his idea of hospitality involved chocolate biscuits and Felix appeared to have more problems than she did. Granny had never given it much consideration before but growing up as a human seemed to be a minefield of 'do's' and 'do not's'. A bit like being a tooth fairy she considered, reaching for the bag of letters.

'Oh, I almost forgot,' whispered Felix. 'There was a lot of gossip in the village the other day, about lipstick on the angels in the graveyard. You don't know anything about that do you?' Granny twiddled with the 'o' in her fingers, reaching for the 'n' on the stand in front of her. She held them up, batting her eyelashes with a smile. 'Me, neither,' Felix agreed, 'I mean, who in their right mind would put lipstick on angels...'

'I have a shrewd idea!'

The voice came from near the window. Felix leapt to his feet, looking wildly for the owner of the voice. Granny stood; plastic letters slid down the folds of her skirts. Watching Granny's brows slip from startled arches to a deep frown, he turned his head to follow her gaze. Two figures stood on the windowsill before his curtains, like actors on an empty stage. Motionless, they were clad in dark gleaming material one black, one in dark blue.

Remembering to breathe, Felix glanced at Granny suspecting at trick. Her face drew back into a snarl,

111

fists clenching at her sides. Looking closer at the figures on his windowsill, Felix noted the masks that covered the faces and the belts slung low about their hips. When a face turned toward him, light flashing off the glass lenses, he leapt back. With a fleeting look at the spiky-heeled boots, Felix shuffled behind Granny on his knees.

*

Colin landed breathlessly. Shaking, he did a leg check. Nine, which was better than seven, he decided madly. Scuttling over the pile of bricks at the bottom of the tower, he dived for the footpath. It was misty down here; the fireworks had left a tang in the air. At the kerb, Colin leapt starting to run across the road.

Out of the mist exploded a car, bright headlights blazing. 'No!!' Colin screamed, rearing up on to his back legs. The car kept coming, the engine deafening as it rolled toward him. Frozen, eyes tight, Colin waited for the squish. A hot shadow, then a boiling wind, he was flipped over backward. The car roared inches above him, spinning on his back Colin wept with fear. Then it was gone. In the silence that followed, Colin lay panting on the tarmac.

Wearily he rose, tottering to the other side. Climbing the kerbstone, he collapsed. What was he thinking? He would be no use to Granny squashed into the tread of some tyre. Resolute, he caught his breath. With more care, Colin stealthily crossed the pavement to the side of the pub. Climbing the wall, he made for the chimney. It was the only way in for a spider.

*

'Hello Marguerite!' said the figure in black, pulling back her hood to reveal a severe dark haircut. The warm skin and tiny features were exquisite, with red lips and turquoise eyes.

'My name is Granny Green Teeth!' hissed Granny

'Still playing silly games I see.' From the windowsill, the stranger looked about her with contempt. Granny flushed but remained silent. In the moment that followed the figure in blue waited patiently, hands on hips. Felix swallowed, he had no idea what had just happened or how they had got in here, but he really hoped they would not tell his Mum and Dad.

'Well now. This is all, nice and awkward,' said the figure in blue. With a dazzling smile, Bell decided to take matters into her own hands. 'Hello Marguerite. Sorry to intrude young man, but we have a bit of business with your...friend.' She pulled back her hood to reveal long blonde plaits.

'You mean Granny?' Felix was confused.

'If you insist, right then....' Bell ploughed on. 'I'm Bluebell, you can call me Bell, and you are?'

'Felix,' he mumbled, glancing at Granny who stared alarmingly at the figure in black. 'I'm Felix.'

'Felix it is an honour,' she said. Bell leapt from the windowsill to the bed landing on the mattress in front of him. 'Before we have a chat with Granny here, I'd like to take a look at your teeth.'

'Err I don't think I want you to.' He prodded Granny in the back. 'Do something.'

'It's all right, she's a tooth fairy,' said Granny. Felix dropped his jaw in surprise. Well, that explained who she was, but he still had doubts about letting her see his teeth.

'I've had some biscuits, so...'

'Just open up, nice and wide. Good,' said Bell, fluttering in front of him with a small torch. Squinting down his nose, Felix was desperate to see her wings. They hummed as she hovered, and a soft wind tickled his face. 'Good to see they are lovely and white.'

'Unbelievable! What are you playing at?' snapped the figure on the windowsill. Surprising Felix, he almost forgot the other fairy was there. She stared haughtily at Granny.

'Scrabble, we are playing scrabble,' replied Granny.

'Don't play the innocent with me, you fool!' The fairy rose menacingly from the windowsill, she hovered in front of Granny waspishly. 'Even after all this time, you have learnt nothing! You insist on....'

'Stop!' Felix hissed loudly. 'Who are you people? And what are you doing in my room?'

'This is a visit from the tooth fairy,' said Granny. Turning to Felix, she pointed to the figure in black. 'And that, is my baby sister.'

Family Ties.

Colin climbed stealthily across the chestnut mantelpiece in the lounge of the pub, cautiously tiptoeing around a gummy ring thick with dark fluff. To Kevin's annoyance, the landlord had started making sticky fruit cocktails; some of the surfaces were a death trap of tacky pineapple juice. Climbing the walls to the back of the bar, Colin was shocked to realise it was quiz night.

'And number five, the correct translation of 'Tempus Fugit' is....'

'Time Flies,' gasped Colin, reaching the top of the bar.

'Time Flies!' agreed the quizmaster.

'Hey, Colin, where've you been spider?' Kevin waved cheerfully. The leggy black spider crawled along the threads that lead to the ornate chandelier in the centre of the room.

'Seriously, you will not believe it,' said Colin, his breath came slower now. A loud bang came from below, the front doors crashed open, silencing him. The force of the wind almost brought down the web line. Dust dropped from the chandelier. 'What on earth?'

gasped Colin. A wild man wearing a tinfoil hat appeared in the doorway. 'Oh, it's Mac Duff.'

'They're coming!' Shuggy Mac Duff yelled from the doorway. 'I know they are coming...' Several sympathetic quiz members rushed to lead Shuggy to the bar, thrusting a drink between his trembling hands. Note pad in hand Sergeant Blomley slowly ducked down. The whole village had been lit up by fireworks. However, for Shuggy it was the work of alien invaders, the Sergeant crawled quickly to the front door

'Your girl's been busy, I see,' said Kevin shrewdly to Colin. Below them, the quiz and the usual chatter resumed.

'Well, you know how it is. Listen Kevin, I need to find that kid's house, something weird is happening.'

'What, more than usual?'

'Yes!' Colin snapped.

'All right, calm down.' Kevin, surprised by his tone, saw how ruffled Colin appeared. Hairs missing and smudges of oil on his legs. 'What has she got you into, now?'

'It's not her, it's someone else,'

'I bet it involves her though.' Kevin frowned darkly.

'Probably, but Kevin, I have to find her.' Colin finished desperately.

'Fine, old Albert's over on the chandelier. You go over, I'll fetch you a wood louse.' Kevin watched his brother inch across the thread, high above the crowded pub.

*

'This will stop anyone from hearing us.'

The fairy in black, scattered glittering dust around the doorframe. Felix was furious, about to speak out, Granny silenced him with her hand. 'All right Asta, what do you want?' said Granny. 'You didn't come here just to say hello, so spit it out!'

'You are right, of course,' said Asta. Standing on the bed, she looked down her nose at Granny. 'I have a mission. Believe me I certainly would not bother...'

'Oh! Give it up, will you.' Granny was livid. 'Let me guess, you wouldn't have bothered because I'm so wicked, but someone had to do it. You are a real hero! Now get on with it.'

'Linden wants to see you,' said Asta.

Granny blanched; her eyes flickered quickly over Felix's blank face. 'So?' she replied haughtily.

'Now, I don't think that is the attitude.'

'He knows where I live, if he wants to see me.'
Granny folded her arms. 'Funny that. You all know
where I live, yet, not a single visitor in twenty-five
years. Some of you used to be my friends.' Her eyes
rested on Bell.

Felix gingerly leant away from her. This was too
much; Granny was not Granny. Her sister was a tooth
fairy. She had never mentioned a sister before, in fact,
there was a lot she had not told him. Although one
thing was clear to him from the way Bell blushed, she
had friends that had let her down.

'You were cursed Marguerite,' said Bell, standing
her ground. 'Nobody would defy the Queen. It would
mean…'

'That, you would be standing up for a friend. Did,
any of you?' Granny's eyes blazed. 'No, I didn't think
so!' Bell raised her chin and endured Granny's stare.

'Enough,' said Asta, sat on Felix's folded duvet
looking highly amused. 'He wants to see you now,
which should be enough. We need to get going.'

'And if I won't go?'

'Then I'll bind you and take you anyway.'

'You wouldn't dare!' Granny raged, looking as
though she might leave the floor herself, even without
wings.

'Please,' Bell called out. 'Do not make her do this. You don't understand what has happened. You have to come with us.' Felix began to feel scared. Asta slowly unhooked something from her belt.

'No.' replied Granny

'Please,' implored Bell. She flew down to the carpet before Granny.

'No. If you lot have a problem, sort it out yourselves. Now leave me alone, I have a game of Scrabble to win.'

'I'm begging you please.'

So, intent on Granny, Bell never noticed Felix grab the slipper. 'Stop right there!' he demanded, glaring at Asta. 'Put that thing down or the fairy gets it!'

'What are you going to do? Make her wear it?' Granny asked Felix, inspecting the novelty slipper trembling over Bell.

'I'm not sure, but she has something.' Felix pointed his slipper at Asta, in her hand was a thin, wicked looking, black rope.

'You wouldn't hesitate, would you?' stated Granny. Asta shrugged.

'Okay,' he said. Felix lowered the ginger monster foot. 'Now, we want some answers. Why does Granny have to come with you?' All three faces turned to Asta expectantly, she twisted the black rope between two fingers.

'Nemesia is missing!' said Asta. Granny gasped, turning away hands over her mouth, slowly the scruffy shoulders started to shake.

'Look what you did!' said Felix.

'Oh please, spare me the dramatics.'

A single tear took the solo journey off the end of Granny's very long nose. 'Priceless! You people are priceless,' she snorted. Felix gaped; she was not crying, she was laughing. 'You come here, not a word for years, then all of a sudden Linden wants to see you! All, because you have gone and lost Nemesia. Not easy to do, I will grant you that. Congratulations to you all, now Get Out!'

'Shush!' Felix was not entirely sure fairy dust would block out that.

'I don't think you have entirely grasped the situation,' Asta replied coolly.

'No Asta, I think it is you who hasn't quite grasped the situation.' Granny poked her with a finger, a spark cracked between them. 'I do not care; I don't have her stashed away somewhere in my stupid tower. She abandoned me years ago, so why would I want anything to do with her or any of you? It has nothing to

do with me. You lost her; you find her, now go away.'
Granny flopped on a pillow.

With a sigh, Bell fluttered across the floor, kneeling next to Granny. 'Just hear us out. We think it has something to do with, you.' she said carefully, 'Another fairy is missing. Yes, the Queen is gone, but it is the hope! We can feel it failing.'

*

In a low building at the edge of town, fluorescent lights flickered into life bouncing harshly off the metal surface below. A low hum thickened the air. Strewn across the countertop were sharp tools of jagged, cold steel, the handles of beautifully cruel pliers lay wide open in front of two glass bell jars connected by heavy wires.

Shockingly loud, a stool scraped across the floor. Nemesia opened her eyes. Turquoise, they glowed with exhaustion, purple smudges lay deeply underneath. Before her, a tanned face smiled showing hard white teeth through the glass that imprisoned her. It's grey eyes appeared triumphant.

'Tell me what I need to know.'

It was little more than a whisper, but she heard it. 'I have told you all I can.' As her voice appeared in his head, the air changed pitch making Nemesia wince inside the glass prison. In the jar beside her, Poppy's wings twitched in pain.

'Then watch, as I find out for myself.' His hand shot from beneath the bench, pressing Primrose against the hard, cold glass. Eyes tightly shut; her pale face was crushed against the surface.

'No!' The noise vibrated louder, making them all cry out in pain.

'Tell me! 'he hissed.

Tears slid from her eyes, spilling heedlessly down Nemesia's face. She forced herself to watch as he lowered Primrose into a silver dish.

*

Cradled in the arms of the chandelier, a huge grey spider with legs that sported knees the size of a knuckle waved a welcome. 'Ah, lad you're late. The quiz, is almost over,' said Albert, his wheezy voice croaking. Around the chandelier, an assortment of the SnickerFord spider population clicked or waved at Colin briefly before turning back to their quiz papers.

Colin's sisters, who regularly made up a team with Albert, moved over to give him some room. 'You're' looking a bit fried there, young man,' Albert observed.

'I hope that witch, is not leading you into bad company.'

'She's not a witch, Uncle Albert,' said Colin. No matter what he told them, friends and family never approved of his situation with Granny. 'I need some help, that's all.'

'Well, you've come to the right place. So, what's up son?'

'I need to find a house in the village,'

'Is that all, what street?'

'Every Street,'

'You'll be a long time trying to find every street, in SnickerFord....' Albert coughed a throaty, wooden chuckle. 'Oh, I'm sorry lad. It gets me right there, oh ha-ha....' He wiped his eyes, studying the lounge for a way to help Colin. 'There is Lamb the grocer, no good there I am afraid.' Colin peered down at tonight's contestants, whilst Albert mumbled gently to himself. 'Mac Duff, he does go past on the high street.' He rolled a questioning eye to Colin.

'Err, no thanks,' said Colin. He had seen enough of Shuggy Mac Duff to know hitching a ride with him would be as difficult as a ride on the broom with Granny. 'No, I need someone, steady and predictable.'

'Right you are, predictable.'

'Number seventeen is leopard,' said Kevin. He shuffled up behind them, legs full of woodlice. 'I knew jaguar was wrong, I told you it was leopard, Sheila. Found what you're looking for bro'?' He passed out the insects. Colin shook his head glumly reaching for a woodlouse.

'I have it!' Albert declared, poking Colin who dropped his insect. Albert pointed. 'There is Ashton, from the main street, he backs on to Every Street. He is as steady as you like.'

'Great!' said Colin. His woodlouse slowly seesawed straight into a sticky, orange cocktail below. Smiling slightly, Colin recognised the blond head that bent forward to sip the drink. 'Where is he?'

The ancient arachnid pointed to a solitary figure by the window. 'But his bike ...' said Albert. '...is over there.' In the hallway, leaning against the floral wallpaper was Mr Ashton's pushbike, complete with handy saddlebags.

A sudden scream from below, told Colin, Mrs Landlord had found his woodlouse. As the drama unfolded, the spiders took full advantage of the break in proceedings, spinning Colin a thread long enough to reach Mr Ashton's bike. Grabbing hold of the line, Kevin stopped Colin before he leapt. 'Be careful Colin, it's a dangerous world,' he warned.

'I know Kevin', but she needs me! Thank you, thank you Albert, and thank you all,' said Colin, and he leapt. The thread of silk reeling through his pincers. As he flew through the air, sweeping across the pub, the spiders watched intently. They groaned together as one. Mid- swing, Colin smacked straight into the back of Mr Lamb the grocer, off to order a takeaway before the rush.

*

'If I go, the boy comes too.'

'No, we are not taking the child with us.'

'Well then, you are not taking me either. What do you say Felix?' asked Granny.

So far, Felix had said nothing as the argument raged on. He was more concerned that his parents might come in and catch him still awake, with two tooth fairies, Granny Green Teeth, and an entire box of chocolate biscuits he smuggled from the kitchen. 'Well, it is a bit late and it's cold out there….and,' he said.

'Don't be silly, they wouldn't fly us there,' said Granny.

'Can't you see the child doesn't want to come? You are scaring him,' said Asta.

126

Felix flushed. 'No, she isn't!' He did not like Asta, firstly because she was bossy and secondly because Granny didn't. It was obvious that there was more to Granny than he realized, but he was not about to let her down now. Granny had been in trouble, and her friends had done nothing. He decided that this was something he knew all about. 'I'm fine to go. Where are you taking her anyway?'

'The National Fairy Headquarters, she has an appointment it is not a trip out,' said Asta

'My diary is full I am afraid. So, unless Felix comes, I will have to refuse,' replied Granny.

Bell interrupted from the bed. 'It would be easier just to let him come,' she said. Felix felt a thrill of excitement watching Asta as she considered the idea.

'Fine,' Asta opened a pocket on her belt. 'Who knows, this maybe more fun than you think.' She flitted over Felix. 'Hold still, this won't hurt a bit.' Scattering him with purple dust, she flung some casually over Granny. 'Come Bell, we shall ensure he isn't missed.' They opened his bedroom door, disappearing deep into the house.

'What was that?' Felix rubbed the powder out of his eyes. His ears popped; when he looked back at Granny, she was taller. 'Wow, what just happened!' The bed was looming over him; his slipper was the size of a sled before him. Granny dusted the last of the powder from her hair.

'They cut us down to size,' she said.

Secret passengers.

Scraping against nylon, Colin clawed to stay on Mr Lamb's raincoat. At the bottom the stitching finally provided some traction, Colin gripped hard. Wildly he looked for the bicycle, Colin spotted a few spokes, a glimpse of rubber tyre, then they were out into the night air. How was he supposed to get there now?

Swiftly, the grocer crossed the car park towards the steamy takeaway that sold Chinese food. Colin dug his pincers into the slippery material of Mr Lamb's coat, wincing with every inch as it squeaked. Finally, he arrived at the collar crawling quickly beneath. The door chimed announcing Mr Lamb and his secret passenger.

'How do Mr Ling, four of the usual.'

'Very good Mr Lamb, any luck tonight?'

'Oh no, it was chaos....'

Colin listened to the banter, thinking hard of a way to get from under Mr Lamb's collar and out of the shop. The electric door chimed. Shoes clicked as feet came close to Mr Lamb. Risking a peek, Colin spotted the brightly made up face of Mrs Landlord.

He saw his chance to get one-step closer to the exit. Bubbly blonde hair cascaded down the back of the

Landlord's, wife. With a grunt, he emerged from beneath the collar and slid to the shoulder of Mr Lamb's coat. Colin ignored the, *be-bah* of the door chimes, as more customers entered the damp takeaway. Total concentration was required to make the leap from grocer to perm.

Gathering himself, Colin watched for his window of opportunity. Mr Lamb turned to greet the other customers. Suddenly, he was right under the nose of Mrs Landlord. Her eyes crossed as she spotted Colin, perched ready to pounce. Glossy lips opened in a silent scream. Raising one gold clad hand, Mrs Landlord swung her purse and attacked. Colin dived for the metal counter, dodging past Mr Ling, he squatted behind a paper bag full of somebody's supper. Mr Lamb took the full force of life with Kevin, as Mrs Landlord pounded the fruit and veg man with her purse. Startled customers rushed to his aid.

'Spider!' howled the deranged woman. 'Where is it?' Brandishing her purse, Mrs Landlord held back the rescuers. Inspecting the trembling grocer, she suspiciously noticed a lack of squashed spider. 'Where is it?' Wild eyed she searched the takeaway.

Colin cowered. Above him Mr Ling, glanced down. 'Blimey, it is a big one.' Lifting the bag in front of Colin, he caught the attention of Mrs Landlord.

'Get it!'

Colin leapt in terror. He dived onto the hot countertop. The purse slammed onto the surface where Colin once stood. Running along the hot metal, Colin squealed. 'Ouch! Hot! Hot! Hot! Hot!' Mrs Landlord dived after him, falling headlong into the crowd of customers soothing Mr Lamb. A glittery shoe flew through the air, landing with a splash in the deep fat fryer. Colin spotted a baldhead near the surface and leapt, hot feet throbbing.

'What was that?' the owner of the baldhead twisted about, curious at the hot tickle. Colin spotted a white hood. Throwing a thread, he shot across just in time, the swinging purse crashed into the bare scalp. Mrs Landlord, a crazy wild haired amazon, emerged from amongst the other customers.

'Hey, what do you think you're doing?' Not waiting for a reply, the bald man's wife swung at Mrs Landlord with an equally big purse. Customers scrambled away. The hooded top squashed against the glass window at the front of the shop. Colin wiped away a patch of condensation and gasped. There, beneath the light of the pub's giant coaching lamp, was Mr Ashton fastening his bicycle clips. He could still make it.

The two women locked in battle, squashed toes with spiky heels. Pulling away from the window, the owner of the white top swirled around. Colin scrambled to one shoulder. The door chimed as more people entered the takeaway. Trapped by the two women wrestling on the metal counter, Mr Lamb and the bald man slumped to the ground.

With very little room to retreat, people shoved. Mr Ling held paper bags of food, high above the women rolling on his surfaces. They caught the innocent with false nails, high heels and the odd swipe of a glittery purse. Stumbling over the legs of the fallen men, somebody fled, opening the door heedless to the rapid chiming. Outside, people gaped at the seething mass writhing in the takeaway window. Colin spotted Mr Ashton mounting the ancient pushbike. Urgently, he measured the jump to anyone in the crowd.

In the car park, Sergeant Blomley was filling out his report. The fireworks exploding about the village were a mystery and nobody could help him, but he felt sure he knew a few of the shrouded figures responsible for throwing them. Decidedly, he packed away his notes for the evening, when the urgent chiming of the takeaway door echoed across the car park. 'Whatever, now?' he sighed. Curiously, the police officer got out of his patrol car, letting Mr Ashton pass slowly by on his pushbike. Through the smudged condensation on the window, Sergeant Blomley saw the battle raging inside.

Colin dived, from shoulder to ponytail, shaven head, and hooped earrings down a line of writhing customers. Spotting the police officer at the open door, he leapt like a gazelle. Catching the numbers on the Sergeants shoulder, Colin flew to doorframe above, searching the street for Mr Ashton. 'What's going on here?' demanded the Sergeant.

Noodles flew through the air. Customers watched, frozen as the supper arched high over their heads. Mrs Landlord, astride the bald man's wife, still held a brown bag that dripped with sauce as it landed. Slowly, the tin tray slid down the Sergeant Bromley's jumper.

'Everything all right Sergeant?' inquired Mr Ashton innocently.

'No Mr Ashton, it would appear that I have been assaulted with Chow Mein.'

Mr Ashton peeked curiously through the misted window. Silently, Colin slid down from the windowsill onto the old man's coat.

*

'Oh no, you can't do that, it's the bathroom next-door!' cried Felix.

A large keyhole grew on his bedroom wall where Bell had placed it 'Not to worry,' she said, 'We won't arrive in there.' Felix was astounded, a door appeared, and it opened into a dimly lit office. Asta strode through beckoning them to follow.

'No going back now,' said Granny, looking down at him. She was much taller than he was, and a lot younger than he ever thought. In fact, nothing seemed to fit right. Her nose was enormous on her face. The only resemblance between Asta and Granny was their eyes, different in colour but both were bright and luminous. Of course, Granny did not have any wings; Felix felt a sudden shudder of worry deep in his stomach. Why did she not have wings?

'Come on, we need to get going,' said Bell, leading him through the keyhole.

'Welcome home ladies!' From behind the desk, a fairy in a dark suit stood removing the glasses from her nose. Long dark hair cascaded down her back, her warm smile lighting up the room. 'Marguerite, I'm glad you came.' Granny was rigid, her jaw tensed as the fairy held out her hand. 'I see.' Not missing a beat, she spotted Felix. 'Hello and who do we have here?'

'Err, I'm Felix,' he stammered. This was unreal. Just where the bathroom should be, was a warm carpeted office, and here he was shaking hands with a fairy, as if she was the headmistress at school.

'She would not come without the boy,' said Asta.

'Ah,' The fairy smiled at them. 'Well, that is understandable after so long, she felt the need of a friend.

'Actually Camellia, I didn't have much choice,' said Granny sourly.

'And neither did we,' replied Camellia. 'I am sorry if this is a surprise, but you will be meeting with Linden in twenty minutes.' All business, Camellia addressed the fairies. 'In the meantime, I suggest you both change. Now, any questions?' Granny opened her mouth. 'Not you. Young Felix, a pair of slippers maybe?' Felix noticed his bare feet. 'This way please.' She led them out into a corridor.

'We will be in the powder room,' said Asta. She and Bell went the opposite way.

'Powder room?' Felix questioned Granny.

'It's where they keep the fairy dust.' She said.

'Wow.' Amazed Felix started to grin wildly. They followed Camellia down a short corridor to a cupboard, from which she produced a pair of slippers. Camellia's wings captivated Felix, the delicate iridescent texture laid flat against her back, he saw every vein and scale this close. 'Can I ask you where we are?'

'Of course,' replied Camellia. 'We are at the headquarters of the British Fairy Embassy; this is Admin and Hope management.' She opened a door to a huge office space, a patchwork of desks and glass partitions across a richly carpeted floor. To the left, a wall of dark windows reached from floor to ceiling. Felix caught glimpses of shimmering lights outside, from the different colours he guessed they were in a city.

'Have you lot moved? This place looks different,' asked Granny, unsure of where she was. Felix did not mind, everything was fascinating, especially since he was supposed to be in bed.

'Yes, we moved. We needed somewhere in the city when we went online. Nemesia felt it was better to keep finances with administration and frankly, I am not sorry we moved from the old place. It could be so noisy.'

'Do you mean money, what do fairies need money for?' asked Felix.

'Well, the money under the pillow is currency and we must get it from somewhere,' replied Camellia

'Can't you just make it out of magic?' he asked.

'No, unfortunately magic doesn't work that way.' Camellia gestured to a pathway across the office. 'Walk and talk, we have a schedule. Now, we fairies are not the bringers of magic, magic is within humans, we tame and deal with magic.'

'So, it's really us that are magic?' asked Felix captivated, as he trotted to keep up. From behind them, Granny snorted.

'Really, that nose could be quite unruly.' Camellia handed Granny a hanky. Fairies sat at desks attending to their work, as the little party passed by one or two glanced up from their screens in amazement.

'Yes and no,' continued Camellia. 'Hope is the basis of fairy magic, when the first humans dared to hope, there we were. Now, when a baby is born the parents are full of hope, that and the teeth, provide us with our tools. Our purpose is to reap and spread hope. Spare hope, to those in need, a little bit of magic for those who have none. The humans, who recognise the magic of the world and embrace it, feel its power most. However, we are magical. Do you see?'

'Sort of,' said Felix. He thought it through. 'So, you can't make stuff out of thin air?'

'No.' Camellia led them past a group by a printer. 'It isn't flash, bang! Rabbit out of hat magic, it's real and like all things real, it has limits.'

'And the money?'

'Sound financial investment.' Camellia tapped her nose. 'You would be surprised at what can be done with the cash that slips down the back of a sofa, this way.' Camellia stopped to look around for Granny, she sighed.

Granny stood frozen by a glass panel. Felix followed her stare to a cleaner emptying a wastepaper basket on the far side of the office. Seconds ticked by making him uncomfortable. 'What's going on? Who is that?' he asked.

'An old friend,' said Camellia. 'Much has passed between them. I will fetch her in a moment.' She reassured him gently. Standing with her head tilted, Granny suddenly reminded Felix of Mum. Embarrassed, he turned away to study a portrait on the wall behind Camellia.

*

Granny's heart pounded, she waited for the apron clad cleaner to turn back. Tilting her head, Granny noted the upturned nose, the curly hair like a wedge. Only, they were not as she remembered. The copper curls were now white, the face lined and wrinkled. Her hands shook as she reached for a duster. 'Blossom!' Granny raced across the office. 'Blossom?' she said. Even to Granny, her own voice sounded hoarse.

The cleaner in the flowery apron turned slowly. 'Yes dear?' Vacant eyes, once clear hazel now smothered in a cloudy film, flickered toward Granny. Blossom's face smiled quick and uncertain, before her mouth turned down again tightly. Knotted, bent hands, plucked at a yellow duster eager to return to work.

'It's Marguerite,' Granny said gently, searching for a spark of recognition in the ravaged features.

'That's nice dear,'

'We were friends,' said Granny, her throat tightening.

'Yes dear,'

'Look at us!' whispered Granny. 'Look at us, now!' The hands twitched feebly at the duster. Blossom turned back to the desk. A dread feeling crept over Granny watching Blossom shakily flap the duster.

'Let her be,' Camellia said lightly.

'How did this happen?' Granny rounded furiously on Camellia, who smiled sadly, but did not reply. Looking wildly for Felix, Granny knew she should never have brought him here. Sweeping away, she strode through the office. 'Stop Staring!' she yelled at a couple of fairies peeking over their monitors. Flustered, Granny sidled up to Felix deep in conversation with a fairy wearing in jeans and hair that reached to her waist in long red tendrils. 'Who are you?' Granny snapped.

'I'm Danny,' she said, holding out her hand with a smile. Granny rudely waved it away.

'A word Felix,' said Granny. 'I want you to go back. This is no place for a child.'

'No,' replied Felix. 'They are really nice, and all this stuff is great. Did you know that this woman here, sorry fairy, was the first ever Queen of the Fairies?' He pointed to the portrait of a black fairy, hair swept into intricate braids, greying slightly at the temples. The face was delicate, almond shaped eyes with sweeping black lashes looked out over the office.

'I know, Queen of Sheba, blah, blah blah!' replied Granny.

'Yeah, I suppose you would. About that?' asked Felix. He thought it was about time she told him what had happened.

'It's complicated,' she replied awkwardly.

'Then I stay,' said Felix. 'We got into this together, so we go home together. It is what friends do.'

Granny spluttered at the freckled face before her. 'Fine, you go ahead; I will be along in a second.' She gestured to Danny, who took Felix into a large boardroom. Granny turned to confront Camellia. 'Who did that to her?' Tell me! Was it Nemesia?'

'It was her foolish friendship with you that brought her to this. Her loyalty to you even, when Blossom knew you were wrong. However, that, was an accident. Nemesia is blameless.' Camellia's eyes filled with tears. 'The child brought it on herself, despite my warnings. You know the limits of the Queen's power; she would never do that to an innocent'

'Limits?' spat Granny. 'You people don't have limits. How did you move from the palace?'

140

'Listen very carefully for once!' hissed Camellia. 'This is crown land, the Rose herself thought it was wiser. We have to move with the times, Nemesia understands that. It is a pity you do not.'

'Send the boy home!'

'You silly girl, the child is in no danger. I do not have time to rearrange things. Now behave yourself! Marguerite, I do not know why you always have to create such a fuss.' Opening the door, Camellia pushed Granny through. She looked to the fairies, wide-eyed at their desks. 'Back to work everyone, we have deadlines to meet.'

*

The clump of Mr Ashton's boots on the hall floor, echoed about his empty house. At the bottom of a saddlebag, Colin blew on his blistered feet. Leaving the bike against the wall in the hallway, Mr Ashton flicked on the kitchen light. Colin listened to the muffled footsteps. Come on, he thought impatiently, why doesn't he just go to bed?

Suddenly, there came a grinding sound, of metal on metal. Colin leant back against the leather, listening to a familiar routine. The thump of a tin can placed on a table, a meaty squish with a fork, the tap on the side of the bowl. The rattle of the back-door opening, and a rush of air came down the passage.

Finally, kissy noises for someone named Sabre, Bubble, Egg, Spot, and Bean. Colin raised a few eyebrows. There were more kissy noises for Marble and Lady Julia. He sighed at the thump of pads on the oil skin floor covering. The mewing of seven hungry mouths sending shivers over his body.

'Cats, I hate cats!'

*

Softly lit, the boardroom held a long table that occupied the centre of the room. Felix rifled through the biscuits on a buffet table at one side. 'Wow, chocolate wafers. Want one?' Granny shook her head, nervously pacing the room.

'Tea?' Danny held up a mug

'No!' Granny snapped. 'How many people are going to be here?'

'I'm not sure,' said Danny. 'This is on a strictly, need to know, basis. So, everyone will be important. Look, I have to leave you here. I'm needed to meet and greet.' She opened the blinds that restricted the view of the office behind them. 'You can watch him arrive from here.' Danny left swiftly.

142

'This is great!' exclaimed Felix in the tense silence. 'Are you okay?' Grunting, Granny waved a hand to indicate she may, she may not be. 'Oh, cheer up! Free biscuits remember.' Felix sat in a chair spinning around for a moment. 'I love these chairs,' he spun a few more times. 'So, who is this Linden bloke anyway?

'Well, I suppose he is the fairy king,' said Granny. 'Only they don't have a king, but he is the Queen's husband, so he's as close as it gets.' She watched the boy, dreading his next question.

'And who are you?' he asked quietly.

'Granny Green Teeth.'

'But they call you Marge...'

'Marguerite, yes I was once, a long time ago.' Granny walked to the windows that looked out over a city. Even to Colin, she had never admitted the truth, not without giving it a quick tidy up. Now she had no choice, it was better she told Felix herself. Maybe they would get out of here with some half -truths still in place. 'I was cursed by the Queen and banished to live amongst humans.'

'Wow!' Felix was stunned. That explained a lot, he thought as the pieces fell into place. The naughty step looked pretty cosy, from where he was sitting. 'That's why you don't have wings? What did you do?'

'I broke a couple of rules, crossed a few lines,' replied Granny Uncomfortable feelings crept up from her around knees. She saw Blossom's face as it ought to have been. 'I may have threatened the fabric of human reality... a bit.' She said awkwardly.

'Cool!' he said, that seemed fair enough. He knew reality was important, there were films about how important it was to not meet yourself going forward, or backwards, or something. Like the electricity meter, you probably shouldn't mess with it. A silence fell between them, whilst Felix considered everything, he didn't know about the tooth fairy.

'Do you know what I have always wondered?' asked Felix. 'What happens to the teeth?' Granny sagged with relief. It seemed Felix was not so interested in the finer details of her crimes. Gratefully she joined him at the table.

'Ah,' she said. 'That's easy, they use them to make the powder.'

'Ew yuck!' said Felix.

Granny laughed loudly. 'What do you mean yuck? The most powerful source of hope is a child expecting a cash reward.'

'Still,' Felix wrinkled his nose. 'They might not be clean.'

Lights suddenly brightened across the room outside. The fairies in the office gathered importantly in a line. From the boardroom, Granny and Felix watched as Camellia entered, followed by a great white shaggy figure. 'It looks like a polar bear,' gasped Felix in wonder.

Fairies moved behind the huge white bulk and the fur was stripped away to reveal an enormous man. Dressed in tight black clothes, with boots that reached to his knees, Felix caught a glimpse of long silver dreadlocks that fell to his waist. 'It was just a coat,' he said. 'He doesn't look so bad. Do you have any idea why he would want to see you?'

'Not really,' said Granny. 'But it cannot be good. It never is when your Dad needs a word.' Felix gaped at her. 'Let me do the talking, all right?' she hissed.

'But that means,'

'Yes?'

'If he is your Dad.... then... your Mum! Oh, you really were bad.'

The cat, the rat and the dentist.

Colin climbed slowly up the rough leather interior of Mr Ashton's saddlebag. His feet still tingling from the dash across the hot counter. It was quiet in the hallway; the only sound was the rattle of Mr Ashton's snore and the regular ticking of a clock somewhere in the house.

Peeping out from under the flap, he looked for the cats. After they had eaten, Mr Ashton had retired to the living room and Colin heard the stealthy padding of cat's paws as they drifted to their favourite haunts about the house. He sighed, knowing the most dangerous part of his journey was about to begin.

At Mrs Boardman's house, Colin had lived amongst cats. Pampered killers who played with their prey before leaving it on the mat, preferring instead, the juicy meat served in glittering bowls. Colin had watched countless tormented furry creatures, finished off with the coal shovel when the cats lost interest.

With legs that shook from exhaustion and fear, Colin settled under the buckle to plan his escape. The door was feet away. However, the letterbox looked stiff and heavy. Peering about, he looked into the gloom, seeing only dirty brown walls and the sticky looking picture rail that sliced through the paintwork. A grubby lampshade hung at an angle, fraying around its metal frame. The once bright tassels undulated in the draft that swept the hall, dragging the tangy smell of greasy kitchen and cats toward Colin. He shivered with distaste.

Straining further, Colin listened cautiously, hearing only the strange counter point between man and clock. Bolder, he climbed onto the mudguard, the cold metal soothing his feet. A lamp in the living room cast a murky glow into the hall. Out of one eye, Colin caught the shape of the knobbly banister rail. Up, he thought, I should go up. Vulnerable in the open, he scrambled over the metal frame, coming to a halt on the handlebars. No cats yet, but it was only a matter of time. They were there somewhere; he could only hope they were too full to bother with him.

*

'Granny Green Teeth,' said Linden, standing in the doorway his bulk filling the frame. 'They have told me this is what you prefer.'

'It is.' Granny's throat was painfully dry. She sat at the end of the table, Felix nervously at her side. Linden strode in followed by Camellia. Others began to prepare the room. The lights turned brighter, and Felix saw how much Granny resembled her father, the sharp cheekbones, the blue luminous eyes. Taller than anyone Felix had ever known, with deep chestnut skin and incandescent hair, Linden radiated power and strength.

'And you are?' asked Linden.

'Felix sir,' he said.

'Van Doore!' said Asta as she entered the room, a sly smile on her face.

'What!' Granny twisted to look at the boy, her palms sweating. 'You never said.'

'You never asked,' Felix replied, suddenly conscious he was the centre of everyone's attention.

'Dear me, when the past catches up with you,' laughed Linden, dropping into a seat at the head of the table. 'I take it you are Bertha Van Doore's boy?'

'She is my grandmother,' said Felix, surprised by this turn of events. Granny fidgeted awkwardly beside him.' Excuse me, how do you know her, sir?'

'I returned something my daughter stole from one of her boys.' Linden nodded to the end of the table.

Felix stared at Granny, horror and admiration caused him to stammer, 'You! ...you stole Dad's teeth.' She nodded slowly, not daring to catch his eye. 'Wow, all this time.' Felix was shocked. He had the answer to his father's tooth problem right there. 'I just can't believe it,' he said.

'It's true,' whispered Granny. 'He had his head under the pillow and I just… you know, sort of took them.'

'Wow,' whispered Felix back. 'You just took them?'

'They said, to take the teeth under the pillow,' she hissed back. 'And yes, I know it was wrong.'

'You did it deliberately?' he asked through the side of his mouth. Granny nodded. Felix grinned, smothering his laughter with a cough.

'And a terrible price was paid,' said Linden. He watched them shrewdly from the other end of the table. 'As good as it is to catch up; we are here for a purpose. Shall we begin?' Around the room, lights dimmed, monitors raised themselves up silently from within the boardroom table, a wall lit up to reveal a huge display screen. Camellia, Bell and Danny took their seats, whilst Asta took charge of the meeting.

'Good evening, to all our fairy representatives,' she said. From the monitors in the table voices replied greetings in many different languages. 'Thank you for joining us at such short notice. As you are all aware, we are searching for Nemesia since her disappearance in Australia last month. Keeping everyone informed of developments is our priority, and so we wish to update you all together on our current findings. Of course, we shall recap for your benefit.' Asta glanced pointedly at Granny.

The large screen glowed, an image appeared, a party of fairies smiling joyfully. 'As you all know, except Marguerite of course,' continued Asta. 'Nemesia disappeared at the wedding of the Australian Ambassador to tooth fairy, Lilac, of the Melbourne district in early September. This is an image captured moments before they collapsed. Danny here, has been able to establish that it was some kind of gas used to subdue the wedding party. Whilst rendering them unconscious, there was no lasting damage.'

'We think it was Nitrous Oxide,' Danny's voice came out of the dark. 'No real damage and in small enough quantity to indicate a person experienced in such gases.'

'No magical being would do such a thing!'

The comment came from a monitor close to Felix. 'No indeed, but more worrying,' said Asta. The image faded; a picture of muddy footprints appeared. 'Were the footprints, in and around the glade, the wedding was organised to specifically avoid any human interaction. The Ambassador had permission several months before the wedding, to isolate that part of the park. However, it would seem that a human was present after all.'

'Could a human find out what was, happening?' The voices on the monitors were outraged. 'Who would do this?'

'At first, we thought there was revolution, or maybe a rebellion about to start,' Linden interrupted. 'However, the magical beings of the world are united. Nicholas in Greenland reports that the elves are stable. There are no current human infractions to our refuges. It seems impossible to me, that anyone in the Council would want to destroy hope and peace, by abducting Nemesia. In light of what we have found, it would seem the source of our troubles, may be a little closer to home.' Linden leant on the table, his eyes coming to rest on Granny's pointy face. Felix bit his lip anxiously.

'Don't look at me, I haven't got her,' she drawled.

*

Mr Ashton was not much of a housekeeper, Colin decided, stealthily clambering the threadbare carpet on the stairs. The walls were very unpleasant. Colin had tried to sidle up them, but the greasy plaster was treacherous, and he was terrified of slipping.

Pausing to catch his breath, Colin considered Mrs Boardman's warm cosy terrace, with a thick cream carpet that stretched luxuriously up the well-lit staircase. Colin had never waded knee deep through dirt balls of hair that choked each step here. Shaking his leg to remove a stray cat hair, Colin felt a wave of sympathy for Mr Ashton.

With a sigh, he reached for the faded carpet, heaving himself onto the landing. The smell of cat was stronger here. Staying in the shadow nearest the wall, Colin could see right into the living room below. Mr Ashton lay on an old green sofa in his grey overcoat, hat still firmly on his head. Ragged snores echoed up the hall, the long beard quivered with each new breath. The lamp beside him cast an eerie glow across the pallid skin. Colin decided he could do with a good bath, although he did hear him clean his teeth in the kitchen earlier.

Stepping out onto the landing, Colin allowed the draft from the upper floor to flow across his body. Heat, mingled with the vibrations of numerous cats ahead, quivered the tiny hairs on his legs. For a second panic gripped him, he almost fled down the stairs.

'For Granny!' Colin allowed himself that whisper.

A sudden burst of coughing from Mr Ashton, sent Colin scampering to the banisters for cover. Pressed against the knobbly wood, his eyes roved the hall. He leant out to see if the old man was all right, Mr Ashton grunted slouching further into the cushions, oblivious to the concerned spider. Colin felt guilty for judging his house keeping skills. After all, the tower was barely cleaner than this. A hopeless romantic, Colin thought Mrs Boardman could do wonders here, and she did love cats.

Something trickled down Colin's leg. Warm and wet it oozed over several feet, a rumble sounded in the air above him. Shaking, he forced himself to look up. Two luminous green eyes glared back down, cracked yellow teeth, leaked stinking saliva from the cat's jaws. The smell itself was enough to suffocate.

Colin leapt, slinging a web. A paw slammed into the wooden flooring, narrowly missing him. The paw swept back. Dirty, ridged, claws scored the wood snagging at his silk. Colin, flung in a high arc, twisted as he flew over the banister rail. The cat had spun him badly. He twirled, dizzy, unable to make out the wall. Slammed into the grubby plaster, Colin fell to the floor. The cat spotted the movement. Hissing rancid spittle, it leapt.

Not waiting to regain his breath, Colin scrambled backward into the shadows, pressing against the dusty skirting board. For a second, the cat lost momentum. The spider had vanished in the dark. Eyes narrowed to seek him out, the cat padded forward. Colin gasped. The cats ears flicked toward the minute sound. Still unable to see him, the cat wrinkled its scabby nose. Pushing back against the wood, Colin willed himself not to run; the beast would have him in a second.

The cat drew nearer, its jaws spilling drool over the grubby carpet. His knees knocked as clouds of fishy stench were puffed all over Colin. The cat sniffed the carpet in front of him. Holding his breath, he looked away. The cat's nose snuffed the skirting board directly above him. Colin stared at the rumpled figure of Mr Ashton lying on the sofa.

Hot, fetid breath blew down across him. Colin tried to look away, but one eye betrayed him and slid toward the creature. More goo oozed from the rumbling jaws. The cat drew back to finish the game. All of Colin's eyes snapped shut. 'No! 'he screamed. There was a thump and the cat vanished. Colin opened a couple of eyes. At the top of the stairs, one long claw still held a few strands of carpet. The thread disintegrated and the paw vanished with a cry. Stunned, Colin stood frozen in a puddle of cat spit.

'She nearly had you there, mate,' said a white rat, stepping out from the shadows. 'You're safe. None of the others will be awake. That one doesn't sleep more than a couple of minutes a day.'

A pathetic mewling drifted up the stairs.

'What did you do?' gasped Colin.

'Just a roller skate on the tail, nothing serious mind,' said the rat. 'She will get loose though. She is persistent that one.' Whiskers twitched at the end of the rat's long nose. Colin shook himself in disbelief.

154

'Steady there, that stuff stinks.' The rat dodged the flying spittle. 'I have somewhere you can clean up, if you like?'

'No. Thanks, but no,' said Colin. 'There is somewhere I have to be.' Colin started across the landing. The rat watched the slimy spider wobble away.

'Hey, nowhere is that important after what you've been through,' called the rat.

'Look! Thank you for helping me but I have to get to Granny,' cried Colin, he wobbled again. 'Granny, I have ...to.' Colin fainted onto the carpet.

Derek the rat picked up the soggy spider with a chuckle. Collecting a small tool bag, he whistled a lively tune as he carried Colin, vanishing through a chink in the wall.

At the bottom of the stairs, angry cries promised great revenge.

*

'A month before Nemesia was taken, this British fairy went missing.' Red hair swept neatly to one side, a sprinkling of freckles across the bridge of her nose. Poppy smiled down from the screen a certificate clutched in both hands. 'Poppy, Tooth Fairy of the Year, she was tipped to become a regional supervisor and one of the few fairy's outside H.Q, who knew details of the wedding.' Asta continued.

'And, my cousin!' A sob startled Felix. Camellia rushed to Danny with a tissue.

'As Poppy was in the habit of filling in her paperwork after her calls, we have no specific location for her disappearance. At first, we did not suspect foul play, because she was due annual leave. Since Nemesia's abduction however, we have gone back over Poppy's case, starting with her patch.' A map appeared.

'Oh look, Snickering!' Felix whispered to Granny.

Asta glared at him. 'Yes, it is Snickering, and we have found some very interesting data in that area.' Both Granny and Felix shifted uncomfortably.

'Not you two,' laughed Linden from the end of the table. 'My team have been down there and noticed some of the wildlife acting out of character.' An image of bats filled the screen. 'I am sure you will agree Countess, this is hardly the flight path of a healthy bat.' Someone answered Linden from a monitor, rapidly with a heavy accent. 'Yes, they do seem unable to navigate,' agreed Linden

'How can they tell?' Felix whispered to Granny

'She is from Transylvania, they know a bit about bats there,' Granny whispered back.

Asta faced the table. 'We cannot feel our Queen,' she said. 'Something is blocking her resonance. We have perceived a low-level disturbance in this area, which may be of concern. A frequency disrupting the atmosphere, affecting the bats is preventing us discovering the source. Emitting from a building here, in the south of the town, until we know the cause we must discount it as simply another anomaly. Sadly, tonight we have another fairy missing. Primrose left only a few hours ago and has not checked in. Her patch neighboured Poppy's, two remote villages and a new housing estate bordering the town. Since Poppy's absence, Primrose has been performing double duty.'

A map of SnickerFord flicked up. Exclamations of anger rang out from the screens. Felix looked significantly at Granny. 'This is where we live,' he said. Granny nodded.

Then the tower appeared proudly upon the screen, Asta continued. 'You all know what this tower is?' she declared. Granny tensed by Felix's side. 'We believe, or at least I feel, that the spread of human belief caused by the curse and containment this tower holds, is at its height in the surrounding towns, villages and cities.'

'You live there!' Felix exclaimed.

'Shut up!' she hissed at him. The monitors buzzed with conversation.

'We can assume that Granny Green Teeth,' Camellia took over, addressing the room. 'Has had the greatest effect on the population closest to the tower. The compulsive cleaning of teeth, to avoid her night-time visits, exceeded all expectations. So, we can assume that the quality of tooth care would naturally improve. We have noted before, that the ripples of this curse had reached the continents even though Granny Green Teeth never had the capacity to travel that far. Her reputation has clearly travelled widely.'

Raising her brows, Camellia glanced at Granny. 'Therefore, who, in all of this could be the subject of a negative reaction? Only those, who care for the nations teeth, those human individuals whose livelihood is ensured by the very care they provide.'

'What is she saying? 'Felix was starting to get drowsy. 'Who is she talking about?'

'A dentist?' Granny asked.

Camellia hesitated for a heartbeat. 'Yes, a dentist or maybe more than one. Nemesia never intended anyone but you, to pay the price for your behaviour. It would seem however, that many people have.'

'This building appears to be the source of the disturbance,' said Asta, changing the images. 'We do not know how it is being created. As you have seen, it greatly disturbs the wildlife and renders us powerless,' Felix, almost missed the image that appeared.

'Hey, that is Mr Fogg's!' he said.

'You know this place?' asked Linden.

'Yes, he is my dentist,' grinned Felix. 'He has always been our family dentist. Actually, Dad told me Nan Van Doore hit him with her handbag when he told her, Dad's teeth …when they…. when they disappeared.' Felix smirked at Granny.

'You're saying you know this dentist?' Asta questioned.

'Well yeah! He is my dentist,' said Felix. Feeling Asta should have at least understood what a dentist was. 'He gives you lollies and stuff. Mum doesn't let us have them because they are too sugary, but Dad says everyone should have a treat now and then. Like on my birthday I got this really big bar of chocolate…'

Granny shook her head.

'Yeah, anyway I don't think that Mr Fogg would steal a Queen. I mean he is too busy now because Sylvia, the receptionist. She doesn't work there anymore. I heard her telling Mrs Butterworth about it, in the bakers last summer. She says they are poor, but they can't be poor, because he just took Mrs Fogg on holiday. Mind you, that might have been Ralph's prize;

he won the newspaper competition, they went for three weeks to Australia.'

*

Mr Fogg pulled tired silk curtains back from the window. Rain had drifted off the hills in a fine mist that trickled down the windowpane. Behind him, Mrs Fogg stirred; she dreamed expensive dreams beneath her eyeshades.

His fist clenched against the cold glass. In spite of everything, this foolish Queen would not do as he wanted. All she had to do to end this, was destroy the green fairy. None of them would tell him where, or how to find her.

'Handbag!' Mrs Fogg sputtered in her sleep.

He grimaced. Ah yes, handbags, shoes, nails, extra bits of hair. Didn't she realise how much all this cost? Of course, she did! Why wouldn't she, she was the wife of the counties best dentist. Mr Fogg eyed the heavy trees before the house, weighed down with rain. Drops fell heedlessly from the webbed leaves, carelessly scattered on the ground, just as she had frittered their money away. Money, he had earned caring, helping.

Now, it was up to him. He could not rely on Ralph anymore; the boy was too old since yesterday's birthday. They had told him that! He had taken teeth, paid all that money to keep the lad quiet and it was useless. Mr Fogg slammed his palm against the glass. Well, he would not let it be useless!

He had discovered their secret. He, Arnold Fogg had found the tooth fairies, and now he knew why nobody needed him anymore. He had captured the Queen and he would make it right. Somehow, he would make her tell him! Then, he would destroy the hideous green monster that had ruined his world.

*

In the surgery, the humming droned on. Through the borrowed glow of the streetlights, Nemesia could see Primrose stretched out between tight wires. The light box across the room, lit the frail outline of a fairy wing that shimmered pitifully. Before her on the metal bench, lay sharp instruments soaked in glittering blood.

Nemesia, her head throbbing painfully, gathered her thoughts. *This had to work!* She did not know how long the others could hold out. Between her palms a faint golden light sprang into life. The hum that filled the surgery rose in pitch. Nemesia winced. Beside her, Poppy's wings flickered feebly in pain. Nemesia gritted her teeth and the light grew stronger, the sound grew louder, she struggled to her feet.

Opening bruised eyes, Poppy rose to her knees, drawn to the familiar glow. The noise in the air became louder; the glow in Nemesia's hands grew bigger. It shook the jars, the windows vibrated. Outside, metal grills rattled. Pliers dropped from the surface of the desk. The fairies screamed in agony. The vibrations tore at the magic within their very souls

Light exploded between her hands and she flung it at the coils above her. It cracked wildly against the glass shell, before hitting Nemesia full in the chest. Hurled to the cold metal surface, Nemesia lay still. Smoke curled gently from her body.

'No!' Poppy cried. Unable to rise, she strained to see her Queen.

The room was quiet again, only the awful hum of the coils.

Making plans.

Colin's mouth tasted strange, opening heavy eyes he saw two bright red spheres. Odd, he thought, we never picked any cherries. The shiny orbs blinked. 'Back with us are you friend?' Blinking himself a few times, Colin could not move. His entire body was stiff; the slightest twitch caused unbearable pain. 'That cat spit has dried out.'

'Oou ahhhh oou?' Colin managed. Moving his mouth was agony.

'Me? I'm Derek,' said the rat. 'I live next door to Mr Ashton. Let's get you washed off and then we can have a proper introduction. Eh?'

'Ess…eeaasse,' hissed Colin

A pink ropey tail flashed past the helpless spider. Stiff and tight, Colin could only listen to the rattles and thumps around him. Derek popped back into view; a ball of wet cotton wool clutched in a pink paw.

'Bingo. Just what we need, nasty stuff this,' said Derek, chatting easily as he cleaned Colin, dripping warm water over the spider's stiff black body. 'It's what he feeds them. I thought, after I unstuck you, you could have a little bath. I'm not too fussy, but that stuff really stinks.' Derek pushed a dish of water up the table. 'In you get.' Colin trudged across to the dish, wincing as the occasional hair tweaked. 'There are some tissues and a pinch of soap for you,' Derek pointed a clawed digit.

'Thank you so much,' Colin wearily lowered himself into the water. 'And thank you for the cat thing.'

Cheerfully Derek shrugged. 'No problem. What were you doing in there anyway?'

'I need to get to a house near here, so I hitched a ride with the man, Mr Ashton,' said Colin. The water felt good, he relaxed a little. 'It all went a bit wrong really. I have to help a friend, and I don't know where she is.' Colin suddenly felt foolish, he could have simply waited on the tower. His dramatic dash across the village was beginning to look a little silly. 'Anyway, what were you doing in there?'

'I go in there every now and then. I like to give them what for, it keeps me fit,' replied Derek.

'You're not a street rat,' he said. Colin looked at the immaculate white coat, the pink paws, his gaze lingered on the startling red eyes.

'No, my girl is away at University, so I get the run of the room.'

Colin noticed the comfortable bed. He was in a light airy bedroom, with bookcases and a large cage at

164

the end of the desk. The cage door was open. 'They let you out?' he asked.

'Yes and no,' said Derek, twirling his tail self-consciously. 'As long as I am back in the cage by morning, when the missus comes to change the water, I'm okay. My girl doesn't mind, but her mum's a bit freaky about me. I pretend to be asleep most of the time.' Chuckling, he aimed a long-toothed grin at Colin. 'You should see how fast she does the food.'

Colin smiled; he could quite imagine. He climbed out of the dish to dry himself off, when a thought occurred to him. 'Do you ever get out anywhere else?' he asked.

'Oh, yes.' Derek replied. 'I go down the street that way, there is a rabbit called Molly a few doors down. She is away at the moment, on account of her owner being an entertainer.'

'Really?' Colin was intrigued.

'They do magic tricks and things. Over that side, my mates Dolly and Valentine have a hutch. They are guinea pigs, feisty them two, always up to something. Over there is the Butterworth's parrot, Lancelot. Nice fella', good conversationalist.' This was not the information Colin wanted, although he was fascinated. 'Who is it you're looking for? Maybe they have a nurtured animal companion, I know,' enquired Derek.

165

'A boy called Felix,' said Colin. 'He lives on Every Street. A friend came to visit him; I need to see her urgently. Do you know him or the house?'

'Know it, come, have a look mate!' Derek leapt from the desk, shot up a chair to the window and swept the curtain aside. Colin arrived at the window to see the backyard of the house opposite. Derek pointed with a claw, 'That's the one, just there.'

'I have to get over there!'

'Not in this weather mate.' Rain dripped from an empty washing line below them. Derek sighed. 'No, I would leave it till tomorrow. It looks like you missed whoever it was, the lights are out. Why don't you sleep here, the night? There is plenty of room and if your friend comes back, you can get over there sharpish' He yawned. 'Besides it's been a busy night what with one thing and another.'

Colin thought about making the journey to Felix's room. He shivered at the dirty weather outside, maybe Derek was right he should stay, after all.......... Colin let out a snore.

'That's right lad.' said Derek, gently covering him with a tissue. "You get some sleep."

*

'Well, if that is all decided.'

'It is not!' fumed Granny. 'You are not going to let Felix do your job.'

Felix slid down in his chair. He had volunteered to make an appointment at the dentist. The fairy's had suggested many ways to do this, but Granny had refused them all. Camellia insisted they needed to find out if Nemesia was there first, but none of them could attempt that. He was getting weary. 'Look,' Felix said quietly. 'It is just a trip to the dentist.'

'Then you'll be going on your own.' Granny frowned at him.

'No, he won't!' said Linden. 'You will be with him. You will go in and find out if the man has your mother and then you will leave. This boy has more courage than you do, he hardly knows us, and yet he is willing to help. What we have here is a situation that needs careful handling and I am afraid, that is very much your job.'

'Yes, but he does not have a reason to go to the dentist's,' replied Granny.

'Then give him one.' Linden smiled archly.

'I know you promised you wouldn't turn my teeth green,' said Felix to Granny.

Camellia banged the table. With a dangerous look she spoke very quietly, 'You promised Felix you wouldn't turn his teeth green?' Two pairs of red cheeks answered her. 'When where you going to tell your friend, that it was not within your power to do so?' Felix was not surprised. He knew Granny well enough now to guess she had lied about his teeth. Part of him admired her.

'We hadn't discussed it,' Granny shrugged. 'Fine, if you want to go, go.' Linden laid a hand on her shoulder. 'You will be going too,' he said

'How do you suppose I do that?' she asked. 'Should we all go to bed early? I cannot get out until he goes to bed. So how does that work then, eh?' She looked blankly at the faces surrounding her. A curious look passed between Linden and Camellia.

'I think that failure to treat Felix's teeth, proves, that there are some rules that can be bent,' said Linden carefully. Granny opened her mouth. 'Shush now! Do not say a word. I want you to go to that dentist and see if your mother is there.' She nodded. 'Then, I want you back here to report. Do you understand?' Granny nodded again. Linden turned to Felix. 'Young man, you have answered many questions tonight. However, all we need is information. Take no risks at this place. I will ensure Granny accompanies you. You have my thanks and the thanks, of the Fairy Nation.' The assembled fairies nodded in agreement.

Felix felt warm and special. They were so grateful, it was only a trip to Mr Fogg's, after all. Linden addressed the monitors. 'Ambassadors, I think we have kept you long enough. As you know morale is dipping here, hardly anyone says, 'Please or Thank you'. The old are left standing on public transport. Something needs doing to rectify this, as we cannot stop your tourist's from spreading this when they return home. Without the Queen in circulation, despair takes the place of hope. We will be in trouble if it spreads. I have contacted Father Time, he feels that it would be a good start to bring forward some of the annual New Year quota, so his office has arranged for you to receive some of your money early, only a percentage mind, let's not get luck happy!'

A murmur ran around the table. A fairy asked, 'Any chance of a few red skies at night up North, they are great for morale. They love a bit of dry weather and it might save me a decent percentage, if the feel-good factor is right.'

Camellia took notes. 'Wonderful,' she said. 'You may have to watch your heather in the spring though. How about some early northern lights, I know they are super for Norway,' she pointed to a monitor close to Felix. 'So, people, let's crank up the luck!' Voices from the screens bid farewell and the monitors slid back into the table. 'We must discuss your course of action tomorrow.' She looked seriously at Felix. 'You must not, do anything that will upset or anger this dentist. I wish to emphasise, that we only need

169

information. You must not put yourself in harm's way, not try to save the Queen.'

Granny groaned inwardly. Did she have to say that? Now he would insist on going, there would be no persuading him out of it later. Felix flushed, he imagined himself saving the Queen and all of fairies being grateful. Ruby could never top that.

'We will be fine won't we Felix? Straight in, straight out,' said Granny, before Camellia could put anymore silly ideas into the boy's head.

'Can we be there at all?' Camellia asked Linden.

'No, we had to move back. Without knowing how the energy field works, we cannot take the chance. Gorse almost had his ears blown out on the driveway. I would like to get the bats away from there, but we just cannot get close. No, I'm afraid you're on your own.' Linden replied.

'Will I be affected in the building?' Granny stood and paced the room,

'I just don't know,' said Linden 'If there were any effects, they would surely be milder.'

'Why?' Felix asked. 'Granny is as magic as you.' He faltered as he looked at the faces round the table. 'Isn't she?'

'You haven't been honest at all, have you?' Asta said, shaking her head.

'No, of course I wasn't,' replied Granny. 'What, did you think that I would see the error of my ways? Did you think cursing me would make me a better person?'

'This is getting us nowhere,' said Camellia. 'Felix, Marguerite was extremely, well, difficult. You see, not just over your father's teeth, there were other things. Granny Green Teeth is controlled by magic, not the other way around. She is no longer a fairy, in effect no longer a magical being in the same sense that fairies are'

'She never said she was magic,' he said, Felix caught Granny's eye. Steadfast, he would not let her down in front of them. 'At least her ears won't explode in the dentist.'

Granny snorted with laughter. 'Now we have established that I am a big nosed, powerless, evil, entity, can we concentrate on the tower?'

Bell hid a smile behind the pages of a leather-bound book. 'I am pretty sure, that we could get you out if Felix went to bed without cleaning his teeth, at any time,' she said. They all gathered about Bell to look at the book.

'No, the magic has never worked in the daytime.' Granny commented, shaking her head.

'You have probably never tried,' said Asta.

'Yeah, thanks Asta, that was really helpful,' Granny sneered. Bell flipped the pages of the book, pointing out various passages of Fairy Lore. Camellia rose from the table, at the large windows she looked out sadly on the city, listening to them bicker.

'Marguerite?' said Camellia

'What!' she snapped.

'Did you ever try the door?'

'No, it is locked. Why, would I try a locked door?' she said waspishly. 'Why, would I try a locked door that is useless and should not be there any…. way.' Granny dropped into a seat, head in her hands. 'No, no, no, no, she didn't? She did? What was she thinking? Did she think I would just go out, get to know humans and love their merry ways? Rescue a few cats. Put out fires. Was she mad?'

'She gave you a way out and 'she' is your mother.' Linden warned.

'It's just open?' asked Granny.

'No, that would be too easy,' said Camellia. 'It would not be a punishment if you could just walk away. Nemesia had faith in you, you the eldest, the brightest of her children. She thought you would work it out, that you would find the humility to leave that prison

However; you are much more stubborn than she realised.'

Granny felt sick and stupid.

'So, she can just leave whenever she wants?' asked Bell.

'No, she must work out how to leave,' replied Camellia.

'And I have to really want to, don't I?' said Granny. 'Do I have to go back, once I am out?'

'Eventually, like I said, it is not a punishment if you could just walk away.'

Granny looked to Felix sagging in his chair. 'Then we will do this,' she said. 'Where is this dentist anyway?' She got up and studied the map, Asta joined her, and they argued over the route. Bell made a list of things they would need for Granny, especially a disguise. 'I want some powders, not just the green one. We need some back up, just in case,' Granny said to Linden.

Linden nodded to Bell. 'Get her what she needs,' he said. 'Only, you will do no harm Marguerite.' His voice full of authority, any warmth vanished. 'Understand!'

'Me, harm never!'

Felix drooped, as they finalised the details. Who would call the dentist? What was Granny's story? He yawned hugely, 'Are we going home soon?'

Camellia smiled, 'Yes, my brave boy. We will take you back now.'

*

Back on the tower, Granny stared down at the tiny village below. Thrashed by diamond hard raindrops, she was lost in terrible thoughts. Rain punished the terraced houses, lashing at windows, beating chimneystacks, pounding slate roofs. Colin was gone, she needed him, and he had left her.

'You know there will be consequences if you don't open that door tomorrow!' The voice cut through the rain. Granny turned, her cloak billowing raggedly behind her. Asta stood before her, rain simply bounced off the tooth fairy.

'Have you got the powders?' Granny shouted against the wind. Asta held up a dark leather belt, numerous pockets covered its length. She threw it down onto the stone before Granny. 'Good, now get off my tower!' sneered Granny. She bent to retrieve the belt,

174

but Asta was quicker, placing a black booted toe on the buckle.

'First, I want to make sure you get this right,' said Asta loudly. 'You might fool them, but I don't think you can.'

'Just how are you going to do that?' yelled Granny, she yanked on the belt. Asta lifted her elegant foot and Granny fell hard onto the stone, she cursed silently. Asta leant forward, lifting Granny up by the jumper, holding her effortlessly in the air. Granny's cloak blew off, escaping into the night. Wincing, as the bunched-up cotton of her blouse pinched, Granny glared at her sister. 'What!'

Snatching her close, in Granny's ear, Asta whispered, 'I know a secret!' Turquoise eyes alight with power; Asta dropped her carelessly, stepping toward the staircase. Granny followed rubbing her chest angrily.

'What do you want?' Granny demanded, in the shelter of the first landing. Colin's books were scattered about the place, the hammock swung in the wind, her rocking chair full of damp paper and toys creaked back and forth. Seeing the tower through her sisters' fastidious eyes, Granny burned with humiliation. Without thinking, her hand swept up to shove Asta over the edge.

175

'Not quick enough.' Asta caught her wrist and thrust her back against the sooty bricks.

'Always worth a try though,' snarled Granny. Chin to chin, she glowered at Asta. 'So, what's the big secret, do you have a key?'

'After a fashion,' smiled Asta. 'You know, I don't think you will ever get through that door Marguerite. You don't want to.' Granny swallowed nervously. She was concerned about that, Colin was not here, and she needed his clear head. 'You will never get through that door, not without knowing the truth,' said Asta, her beautiful face cocked to one side as she examined Granny's ravaged profile.

'So, you trust me with this,' said Granny, lifting the belt. 'But you don't think I can get through a door?'

'I don't trust you at all,' laughed Asta. 'If you were really the brightest of us, you would already know the truth.'

Granny grinned. 'That really bothered you didn't it?' she said with a knowing smile. 'And what is the truth then?'

'Blossom!' Asta whispered. Granny clasped a hand to her chest, pulling away from her grasp. Asta knew that gesture well, Marguerite would never face anyone unless it was to mock or laugh. Angrily, Asta grabbed Granny's arm, 'Don't you turn away from me!' This time Granny was fast enough and with her free hand, she slapped Asta hard across the cheek. The slap rang around the tower. Asta raised a hand to her livid cheek. 'Maybe if you knew the truth, you would do a bit of soul searching.'

'I already know the truth,' Granny spat. 'She cursed her! She blamed her for what I did and cursed Blossom too. Our mother, Queen of all the Fairies, Defender of the Cause, cursed her for nothing. You say you know, but you do not! You were not there, Mummy's precious baby, you know nothing!'

'I know a lot more than you. Nemesia did not curse her, Blossom cursed herself.'

'Yes, in her choice of friends, I've already heard it. Go away.' Granny started down the stairs.

'No, you fool,' she said. Seizing Granny, Asta forced her to listen. 'Nemesia was devastated. You alone were supposed to be the one to pay the price for what you did. She knew Blossom had tried, that you were the leader. She tried to make you a good tooth fairy, but you were too arrogant.' Granny struggled to free herself, dropping the belt. 'Your dislike of our service to mankind, threatened the very core of our being. They needed to stop your ideas from spreading. You, not Blossom!'

Granny tore herself away. 'Shut Up!' she screamed, dashing down the steps she stuck her fingers

177

in her ears. 'Shut up, shut up.' Hurtling deeper into the tower.

'Blossom defended you,' said Asta. Sailing down the centre of the tower, fluttering wings holding her effortlessly over the black drop. 'Pleaded with Nemesia, promised to be firmer, but Mother knew it had gone too far.'

'Go away!' Picking up a crumbling brick, Granny hurled it at the fairy.

'That night, the night she was to curse you.' Asta continued, her voice relentless. 'Blossom begged Nemesia to reconsider. Camellia locked Blossom in her room.'

'Stop it!' Granny tripped, falling down the steps, she landed in a heap.

'Blossom escaped. She went to the powder room and took a keyhole in defiance of the council and it's ruling.'

'Stop it,' she said. Granny's voice little more than a whisper, she buried her face in her wet skirts.

'Blossom entered the room, as Nemesia cursed you. She caught part of the curse, trying to save you. You! Her best friend. What a price she paid for your friendship.' Asta shook her head and asked, 'Do you think it was really worth it?'

She beat her wings and skimmed up the tower, leaving her sister sobbing in the dark.

Telling Lies.

Felix was warm, soft, and comfortable.
Stretching his toes under the duvet, he noticed sounds
drifting up from the kitchen below. Under his pillow,
Felix's hand closed on something crispy. Bolt upright
he read the paper,

After School, go to the playing fields. Do not be
late, I will turn your teeth green!

Granny Green Teeth.

Felix carefully folded the note and slipped it into
his pyjama pocket. He was amazed, had it all truly
happened? How come he was not sleepy? Felix shot to
his feet by the bed, what was it they had done to Mum
and Dad last night? A soft clinking from down in the
kitchen told him one of them was awake, dashing
across the landing Felix bounded down the stairs.

'Felix, slow down,' whispered Mum, narrowly
missed him with two hot cups of tea.

'Hi,' he said awkwardly. Well, she looked fine,
the right size and everything.

'Hi yourself, you're up early this morning,'
said Mum, starting up the staircase. 'Get yourself some
cereal, I was just going back up, it's only a quarter to

180

six you have ages yet. Ruby is still asleep. I had such a good sleep; I must say I did need it.' She breezed upstairs leaving Felix in the kitchen.

Memories of last night, flooded back. He could not believe what he was going to do today. Maybe, he should tell Mum and Dad? No, then he would have to confess about Granny. It all seemed so far-fetched.

He had never gone off on his own before, suddenly telling Jamie he would not be at chess club tonight was not so simple. Jamie's Mum always picked them up. What if this was a dream or a trick? He pulled out the note, wandering aimlessly about the kitchen.

This was going to be a lot more difficult for Granny, than it was for him. He made up his mind, if she did not show, he would get the bus home. He might have a bit of explaining to do, but he could always say he forgot. Grabbing a box of cereal, Felix clanked about in the kitchen. Nerves made him clumsy and he dropped his spoon with a clatter. There was a hiss from the top of the stairs.

'Felix, keep it down you'll wake Ruby,' shushed his Dad.

'Sorry!' Felix hissed back, letting go of the cupboard door so it banged. 'Oops.'

Later, Felix stomped to the bus stop, his insides a jumble of excitement and fear. The rain had washed autumn leaves into damp clumps around the gutters. Morning, sunshine warmed the ginger brown mounds, releasing a sweet, organic mustiness over the village. Crossing the main road, he looked at the tower. It loomed over the village and suddenly he noticed how massive it was. Felix strained his eyes against the morning sun, trying to catch a glimpse of Granny. There was no sign of her. He touched the crispy paper in his trouser pocket, for luck.

*

Mr Fogg unlocked the surgery door; sun glinted off the glass panel as it opened. Snapping up the blind, he felt elated. The dark thoughts that kept him awake late into the night were banished. Today was the day. Opening the appointments book, he ran a long finger down the lined page, empty. Perfect! Snapping shut the book; he took off his coat and placed it carefully over the chair. Smoothing down his grey hair, Mr Fogg walked down the corridor to Surgery No.1

*

Her fingers drew little circles on the dark leather, bloodshot eyes stared at nothing. Granny had let the past sweep over her, a storm of memories, flashes of right and wrong, lightning in her mind.

Trembling, she stood on unsteady legs and slowly descended into the warm depths of the tower. Granny surveyed the webs Colin had made. They had once shone with a cosy glow, now though they were dirty candyfloss covered in cheap glitter.

Wherever he was, it was not here, she was on her own. Reaching along the belt Granny took out a pinch of fine yellow powder, with a last look at the pinprick of blue sky above, she flung it in the air. Golden light flooded the bottom of the tower, she covered her eyes against the sudden brightness. Through parted fingers, Granny saw the door she had ignored for almost twenty-five years.

Two hours later, she had worked up quite a sweat. Pink faced, Granny stood in shirtsleeves, the belt about her hips, fuming at the solid oak door. It bore new scuffmarks and some interesting footprints where she had lost her temper. Through narrowed eyes, she studied the doorway. The bricks arched elegantly over the dark wooden door. Tiny little rows of dogtooth carvings separated each row of bricks. She blinked and blinked again.

'You have got to be kidding me!' Between the rows of brick, the language of her childhood stood out, fairy runes were woven into the pattern. Granny shook her head. 'Great, you couldn't make it simple, could you?' Some of them she remembered, most of them she did not 'You see!' she exclaimed to no one. 'This is where riddles get you, you need me now and the door won't budge.'

Although, it would not be in the way if I were not here, she admitted to herself. A shimmer caught her eye. It was there, only faint but she was sure it was a glimmer. Watching, waiting, Granny snorted with frustration. It was probably her imagination. Closing her bruised eyes, Granny sighed, hoping Felix was doing all right. A little part of her regretted involving him, she did not really think this dentist was dangerous. However, it might be safer alone.

Flash!

Even through closed eyes, Granny saw that. Inspecting the door closely, Granny kicked it one more time. She closed her eyes and thought about Felix.

Flash!

'That is so unfair!' she groaned. Granny forced herself to think about Felix, Colin, and Blossom. The burgeoning golden light warmed her face. Keep thinking, she told herself. Hard thoughts and then one about Asta popped up. The light dimmed. 'No!'

Not tying her wings together and pushing Asta over the edge. Breathing deeply, Granny tucked away that

184

particular regret for later. With her eyes tightly shut, beads of sweat ran off her forehead. She did regret things, not being a better sister. The heat began to scorch. Not, being a better friend. The light blazed so brightly it was white. There was a clunk and a scraping sound. Through one eye, Granny saw the door open a fraction. Above the runes glowed.

'Let your conscience be your guide?' Granny read in disbelief. 'Oh, where does she get this stuff?'

The door swung open wide at her touch, steam poured out of the doorway into the frosty sunlit morning and Granny was blinded by the daylight. Shielding her eyes, she breathed in all the fragrances of the village. The sweet smell of autumn, pies from the bakery, frost that seared the back of her nose. Freedom!

She pulled on her clothing and stepped forward grandly, into the village. Only, her foot missed the step and her tall frame crumpled with a surprised squeal. Every brick that surrounded the base of the tower, connected with some part of her bony body. She groaned. rolling to a ragged halt on the flagstone pavement.

'Pride comes before a fall, you know,' said a voice from above her.

'I was aware, yes!' snapped Granny. Bell wiped her eyes with a tissue, before she gave in to another fit of the giggles. 'Where have you been?'

185

asked Granny. She frowned at the tiny figure perched on the wall by the pub.

'Waiting here for you, I've hidden your disguise in the woods, but we need to make that appointment soon.' Bell flitted to her shoulder. Granny rose with a stagger and scurried across the road to the safety of the telephone box.

*

'Eleven arrests!'

The papery rattle under the Sergeant's nose made him flinch, the report sheet was swept away to join others on the desk. Heat rose up from his knees settling into his cheeks, flushing them puce. Suddenly, the room was very small.

'Eleven! That is virtually a riot man. My cells are full of Mr Ling's best customers, all charged with assaulting an officer with takeaway food.' The Superintendent was on his feet now, his moustache danced with agitation. 'It is a village, YOUR village Blomley!'

The Sergeant crossed his eyes, trying to watch the finger pointing at his nose. 'Broken bus stands, vandalised angels, fireworks, not to mention the squad car.' Notes waved vigorously. 'There is a crime wave sweeping that valley, Blomley. Mrs Van Doore has complained, do you understand? Bertha Van Doore!' Wild eyed the Superintendent held up reports crumpled in his fists. 'Now, I want you to find out just what is going on there, and put an end to it, do you hear?'

Sergeant Blomley nodded. He shot out of the office, to the safety of the new patrol car. Giving it a guilty buff, he clambered inside, ears still smarting from the morning briefing. Something was going on in that village; things were getting out of control. Well, he would find out what it was and 'put an end to it'. Round face set into a determined frown, he started the engine, it purred into life. The Sergeant turned on the powerful heater and enjoyed the blast of hot air. Not everything had turned out so badly, he considered.

*

His maths lesson faded into the background. Felix thought about what was to come, a knee jerking bolt of anxiety shot through him. Clutching his pen, he still had to tell Jamie about chess club. Glancing at his friend scribbling down a problem from the board, Felix opened his mouth. What should he say? He had to be casual about it. Plagued by doubt he fiddled once more with his pen, looking out over the icy sports field for inspiration. The bell rang, shocking Felix back to reality, he had not done any work.

'Hurry or we'll never get any hot chocolate!' Will poked Felix in the back with a ruler. Ramming his books into his bag Felix followed the other two,

'Jamie forgot to tell you, I'm not at chess tonight, Mum is meeting me,' said Felix, telling his lie.

'Great, so you're abandoning me to Amelia, thanks,' said Jamie with a grimace.

'You know her moves. You should be okay.' Felix patted him casually on the back. They dived into the stream of pupils heading for the hall.

'Like that's going to make a difference, you don't have to live with her,' said Jamie, they halted. A chorus of disapproval rang out from the flood behind them. 'No, I'll be losing for sure tonight. I like my life thank you.'

'Don't make it too obvious, she's not that good you know,' advised Will, dodging a group heading for the cloakrooms. Relieved that Jamie was more concerned with Amelia, than with his reason for not being there, Felix let the wash of pupils carry him away.

By the wall of the office, he waited for the others to catch him up. Will, bag tangled with a pupil from the class next door, was struggling to untie it. Jamie, risking his fingers hunted for the money Will had dropped in the collision. Glancing through the legs of passing students Felix spotted the shiny coin, kicked by anonymous feet up against the wall.

'Jamie, over there!' said Felix pointing to the side of the corridor. With a thumb's up Jamie plunged back into the sea of passing legs. He was not the only one to notice, from the dark shadowed corridor loomed the great silhouette of Archie Burton. Pushing Will aside, Archie waded after Jamie across the corridor.

With a whoop of triumph, Jamie held up Will's money. A huge ham like fist clamped down on his hand crushing his fingers. 'No!' yelled Felix. He struggled back up the corridor through the rush away from Archie. Will dashed to help. grabbing Archie's blazer, pulling hard.

'Leave it Burton that's my money!'

Jamie's face contorted with pain. 'Get him off me!' he managed through gritted teeth. Felix grabbed one of Archie's fingers and yanked it back. Archie swung a huge palm at Felix, knocking them all into a struggling ball on the floor, leaving Archie free to admire the coin in his hand.

'I believe that, is Will's.' Nathan picked the money out of Archie's massive palm. The three of them struggled apart. Embarrassed, they rose and straightening their uniforms. 'Typical!' Will muttered.

'You owe them an apology, Burton,' said Nathan.

'I don't think that is necesschary,' slurred a voice.

Looking up in surprise, Felix pulled his tie too tight. Ralph Fogg was smirking at them all from the darkest shadow of the corridor. Felix thought his heart would explode it beat so rapidly. With hands that trembled, he drew down the knot slowly to cover his panic. Mr Fogg's grandson stood before him.

Felix suddenly wanted to shout it out, to tell them all about the fairies and Granny, about the mission this afternoon. Nathan could help, they all could, but...his heart plummeted, he could say nothing. Felix gritted his teeth in an effort not to scream. In the tension between these titans of the schoolyard, they all shifted nervously.

'What hash he got to apologishe for? The shtupid little kid dropped it, he wash helping. Weren't you Arschie?' Felix frowned, what was wrong with Ralph's voice?

'Stealing from kids, that's a new low, even for you Archie,' said Nathan.

'Shhut it Walker! He doeshn't need money. But if you are a bit shhort, here!' said Ralph, he threw a handful of coins at their feet. 'You can have my shange.'

Felix looked hard at Ralph's grinning mouth. He only had front teeth, where his large conceited face split; Felix could see livid pink gums. Grabbing his

190

own bag with shaking hands, he vaguely heard the conversation going on around him. Watching the two figures disappear into the packed hall, Felix was certain he knew how the dentist had captured the missing Fairies.

*

In the surgery, the telephone rang.

Ring, Ring.

Ring, Ring.

Ring, Ring.

It rang over and over again.

Ring, Ring.

Ring, Ring.

The wooden desk vibrated. In the corner of the room, he stood and stared.

Ring, Ring.

A gloved hand reached out with a tremor.

Ring, Ring.

Ring, Ring.

He snatched it up, sweat trickling down his forehead.

'Hello?'

'Hello…... is that Mr Fogg?'

*

Perched on a pile of reference books, Colin was doing the crossword, one eye magnified hugely by a pair of glasses. Despite the bright sunshine outside, a table lamp illuminated the desk casting a warm golden light on them both. Derek seated on a cotton reel, busily cleaned a set of darts, helping Colin with some of the more tricky answers.

When he had first awoken, Colin had been desperate to get to Felix. However, Mr Ashton's cats regularly patrolled the alley. Derek had advised waiting for the cover of nightfall. If Granny appeared at Felix's window, he would have plenty of time to get over there. Feeling a little silly at his own dramatic dash across the village Colin chose to wait. After all, she was probably fine without him.

In the alleyway, Lady Julia eyed the window from the roof of a neighbours shed.

A trip to the dentist.

'PSst! Psst!'

Felix spotted green wellington boots jigging in the roots of the beech hedge that marked the end of sports field. 'Psst!' Checking the vast open space for anyone who would notice, Felix stepped a little closer. 'I said PSST!' Granny shouted.

'Yes, I heard you,' Felix anxiously snapped back. He was cold and resentful, frowning he addressed the hedge. 'Come out. I can see you.' His feet were damp, and his toes were numb. Leaving the crowd on the way to the bus stop had severely tested his nerves. The frozen sports had field made him feel small and exposed as he hurried across. With every pace, Felix had expected someone to shout his name. Terrified and anxious, soggy socks only made it worse.

'How do I look?' asked Granny. Wellington boots and a tweed skirt replaced her old shabby outfit. She had a green and gold headscarf firmly knotted under her chin.

'Fine,' said Felix. He eyed the wellingtons enviously.

'Really?' The troubled frown that creased his forehead caught her attention. 'What's wrong?' asked Granny. Felix rubbed his hands in the afternoon chill, unsure where to start, he chose his feet. 'Well I can fix those,' she said. Undoing her jacket, she revealed the belt.

'Wow,' said Felix. Eager to see what the fairies had given her, he edged closer. 'Have you used any yet?' The contents glowed deep and rich in the afternoon light. Granny rummaged through the pockets.

'Only a bit,' replied Granny, as she flung a pinch of amber glitter at his feet. There was a flash, an itchy crackle, and warmth flooded into his shoes.

'I have something important to tell you,' said Felix. Listening intently, Granny frowned, while he told her about Ralph's teeth. 'He must have used the teeth to catch the fairies.' Felix concluded. 'I didn't know the tooth fairy would show up for teeth you had taken out as well.

'They don't advertise that bit,' she said. 'Felix, you can still turn back, I can go alone.' The thought of the dentist, taking Ralph's teeth concerned her almost as much as how he had wilfully cheated the honesty code.

'No.' Pale faced Felix set his chin determinedly. 'Just do my teeth and let's get on with it before Mum and Dad find out.' His heat beating wildly, he closed his eyes as she reached for the emerald powder.

*

The sound of the vacuum cleaner droned up the corridor. Mr Fogg tidied the treatment room. Shifting gleaming instruments from one tray to another, he glanced at the clock for the hundredth time. Rushing once more to the door at the back of the surgery he tried the handle. Satisfied it was still locked, his fingers brushed the key within his chest pocket.

The sudden silence from the corridor alerted him.

'You can put this away yourself. My hair appointment is in minutes.' Mrs Fogg shouted from the reception. 'Don't forget, the guests will be at the house for seven, you can't keep a soufflé waiting.' Mrs Fogg went on. 'Don't be late.'

'No dear.'

Her heels cracked a hard tattoo on the drive, and she was lost in the gloom of the afternoon. Mr Fogg felt a thrill. Soon, his first patient in six months would be here. A name in blue ink stood out against empty lines in the appointments book. Felix Van Doore 4.30. Tracing the name with his finger, he let out a happy sigh. In the mirror by the empty fish tank, he smoothed down his grey hair. Smiling, he felt like his old self again.

*

They stood at the bottom of the drive.

'This tastes awful,' said Felix. He grimaced, running his tongue over the gritty bumps and ridges of his newly green teeth. 'Are you sure it looks good?' he asked again.

'It's fine!' Granny snapped.

'Oh, by the way I brought you this.' Reaching into his school satchel, Felix handed her a brown leather handbag. She frowned. 'For the disguise,' he said. 'So, you look more like Nan Van Doore. She always has one.' In answer to her raised eyebrow, he explained. 'She gave this one to Ruby, I took it this morning.'

'Well, everything is just fine then,' said Granny. She hoisted the bag on her shoulder and breathed deeply. 'Come on let's get in there before we both run away.'

'Don't be a baby it is just a visit to the dentist,' chuckled Felix nervously.

*

Inside Mr Fogg hummed a happy tune. Checking the clock over the reception desk, he noticed it was running slow. Silly, he had been letting things slip. As he climbed up to move the hands, the door swept open and his patient arrived

196

'Felix, my boy how wonderful to see you.' Leaping down, eagerly Mr Fogg approached the two figures at the door. 'You caught me out there, but we simply must have the right time.' In his enthusiasm, he shook Granny's hand. 'And you are?'

'Great Aunt, Agatha Van Doore,' Granny replied stiffly.

'Ah, yes,' he said, stepping back. Granny's willowy height registered a family resemblance. Before he could focus on her nose, she strode past him inspecting the waiting room with an arrogant air that only reinforced her Van Doore credentials.

'And you, are Mr Fogg,' she declared.

'Yes, yes I am.' Mr Fogg smiled at Felix.

'Well, you come highly recommended,' she said, subjecting a framed print of delicate pink flowers to close scrutiny. With a modest nod, he shepherded the silent child into the drab waiting room.

'I have been the family dentist for many years now.'

'So, Bertha told me.'

Mr Fogg glanced at Felix. Well used to the pomposity of his grandmother, Mr Fogg expected nothing more from her sister. However, Felix was strangely quiet.

'How is Mrs Van Doore?'

'Oh, you know, in the pink as usual.' Granny turned. Mr Fogg looked into her eyes first and then noticed her nose. He tried to look away, aware he was staring.

'I.'

'Yes?' She queried; head cocked to one side.

'You don't live around here,' said the dentist. He gave Felix to a look of great sympathy. Bertha Van Doore was a handsome woman, in her own way, but this aunt was hideous.

'No.' Granny replied, 'I live in London, the boy has been staying with me.' Her sharp memory recalled the details she had rehearsed with Bell. 'Yes, he was quite horrid to his sister. Weren't you Felix?' Felix had not expected that, and he glared at her.

'Well, I think we should see what the problem is,' Mr Fogg interrupted.

'Yes, as do I. Show Mr Fogg, Felix,' demanded Granny. Felix shook his head, mouth firmly clamped shut.

'Come now Felix,' the dentist cajoled.

'Show Mr Fogg boy!'

Mr Fogg looked at Granny sharply. 'I don't think that is necessary,' he commented, missing the furious glance Felix gave her.

'Fine, have it your own way,' said Granny. She sat in one of the wooden chairs lining the room. 'But he is a stubborn one that boy.' She gestured at Felix with the handbag; Mr Fogg caught a spark of something familiar.

'I am sure that this will be nothing, may I have a look Felix?' said Mr Fogg gently. Behind him, Granny winked quickly. Felix swallowed, slowly he opened his mouth and revealed the stained green teeth. With horrified fascination, Mr Fogg stared at them. 'Felix,' he asked in a whisper, 'How did this happen?'

Possible treatments collided with counter treatments, leaving no room for doubt or suspicion in the dentists mind. The beating heart of a professional care giver thudded into action.

'To the surgery immediately, this will require de-scaling, polishing.' Mr Fogg led them to Surgery No 1. 'He has been cleaning them?' asked the dentist, eye to eye with Granny in the doorway. She never flickered, meeting his gaze with ice-cold contempt.

'So, he says. Though, I am not in the habit, of interrogating children.'

'Well, I'm sure there is plenty we can do,' said Mr Fogg. 'Into the chair Felix, you know how.' Granny stepped into the room. Every hair on her head lifted, she wanted to scream, a metallic tang tasted in her mouth. In the chair, Felix saw her panic.

Mr Fogg busily fitted his mask, selected a mirror and hook from the tray at his side, adjusted the enormous spotlight and happily requested that Felix, 'Open wide.'

'My goodness!' the dentist exclaimed for the tenth time. 'You say the water is good?'

Granny twitched. This was taking too long. The smell of disinfectant was getting up her nose. 'He may have allergies!' she said. A piece of green tartar snapped off and pinged onto the surface behind her.

'I'm afraid I may have to drill some of this off.'

'Fine,'

'No way,' said Felix.

'Do you want to explain all this to your grandmother?' Granny asked sharply. Felix just wanted to go home.

'It's for the best Felix. I'll be as quick as possible,' said Mr Fogg.

Putting down the scorching drill, Mr Fogg pulled down his mask in frustration. 'I'll have to get some more tips; these are not quite doing the job,' he said.

'Are you all right Mr Fogg?' she asked. Granny tried to look sincerely concerned.

'Fine, yes. I just need to fetch some... other things.' He passed the back of his hand over his forehead, pulling off his rubber gloves. 'I think I know just the thing. You stay here.' They could hear him speaking as he went. 'In the store's I think....'

Granny leapt to her feet.

'Quick,' Felix whispered. 'Look for something, anything so we can get out.'

'Watch the door!' she said. Granny stood in the centre of the room for a moment, drawn to the doorway at the back of the surgery she touched the smooth wooden surface. Fascinated, she watched as the hairs on the back of her hand stood up. A crash at the end of the corridor startled them both.

In the store cupboard, Mr Fogg had remembered something important. That handbag! A box of drill bits lay scattered at his feet. In the light of a single bulb, he remembered that handbag and knew it. A tiny spark of recognition smouldered into a blazing image, of the boy with no teeth. He shuddered. From that day, nothing had been the same.

Head spinning, Mr Fogg clutched the shelves, his fingers tightened on the wood. He swung his head, the corridor rippled before him. That woman with steely blue eyes, he dug painfully into the wood with his nails. Her nose was the last piece of a puzzle. A tiny voice, shrieking in agony, rang inside his head. 'She smells them!' screamed the fairy. 'She smells them out, with that enormous nose.'

'I KNOW YOU!!!'

His roar thundered down the corridor. Granny slammed the surgery door shut. With a finger pressed to her lips, she thought for a second. 'I think we might have been rumbled,' she said.

'You think so?' Felix stood white faced, looking at her in disbelief. 'Maybe he just met someone he knows at the end of the corridor.'

'I do not think now is the time for sarcasm. Get ready to run,' she whispered quickly.

A loud booming travelled up the narrow dark passage. Mr Fogg had stumbled witlessly into the storeroom door, his lanky figure crumpled falling to his knees. 'GRANNY,' Mr Fogg yelled. 'GREEN TEETH!'

'I'd say he knows who we are.'

Shelves broke as the dentist dragged his long frame upright. She had come to him. Now he would end this, everything would be all right again. He would destroy her, thought. Mr Fogg staggering down the carpeted passageway.

'Seal the door,' hissed Felix. There was a muffled groan from outside. Granny opened the belt and tossed some powder at the door to the corridor, it burst into flames. The flames disappeared as quickly as they had arrived leaving tarnished orange glitter on the floor. 'You used that on my feet!' exclaimed Felix. Spinning the belt around her waist, Granny fumbled with the pockets. 'Do something, now!' he demanded.

'Just give me a second.' Granny started to sweat. Mumbling drifted to them from the passage.

'I know you............ who you... are,' panted Mr Fogg. Limping, he leant heavily against the wall. Reaching down, he pulled a drill bit painfully out of his knee, dropping it on the floor. Blood smeared the wallpaper under his fingers.

'What's the opposite of green?' asked Granny.

'Yellow? No... blue. Blue,' said Felix, he caught her meaning and started to pull at the belt.

'No,' exclaimed Granny, slapping his hand away. 'The OPPOSITE!'

'Why don't you know?' asked Felix.

'I've gone blank,' she said.

'What now?'

'Yes, now,' she barked. 'I'm not sure.' Granny flexed her hands indecisively over the open pockets. Another thump against the wall, closer now.

'I don't know,' squealed Felix.

'Think!' she shouted.

Felix backed into the chair shaking his head, every footstep crunching up the pieces of tartar that covered the floor. 'I don't know, I don't KNOW!' Felix looked helplessly at Granny. Her cheeks were flushed with panic. 'Red,' he said quietly to himself.

'What?'

'Red. It's the red one!' he yelled. The handle twisted into Granny's spine. Jamming a foot against the bottom of the door, she span, throwing a shower of glittering red over the door. Flinging herself at Felix, she scooped him up and dived behind the chair.

It was silent for a moment. They each held their breath, hoping that the door would hold fast. Then the banging started. Sat together against the bottom of the chair, they clutched each other tighter with each mighty crash of the door.

Outside, Mr Fogg pounded on the surgery door with his fists. If they found the Queen, they would release her. Panic drove him back, retreating down the corridor to another examination room. A metal cabinet stood in the far corner, padlocked. He dragged open drawers, slinging them across the room. A set of keys fell to the floor.

'What's he up to?' hissed Felix in the silence. Granny shrugged. Crawling across the surgery floor, she sprinkled more red powder onto the lock.

'Just in case,' said Granny, she crawled back. 'That was close.'

'I knew this was a bad idea. We shouldn't have come here,' said Felix. He was very worried.

'That's not what you said last night,' she remarked, studying the windows above them.

'Yeah, well, what do I know? I'm twelve,' he said. Granny snorted a chuckle. They sat listening to the muffled sounds of the dentist further up the corridor.

'How are we going to get out?' asked Felix in a small voice.

'If I'm not mistaken, what we need is in there,' said Granny, nodding to the wooden door at the back of the room. Felix regarded the flat polished surface, it loomed with mystery and opportunity.

'Not out of the window then?' he asked.

'No, not out of the window,' she replied. Granny stared grimly at the door. 'We have nowhere else to go.'

'Arghhh!' yelled the dentist, charging at the surgery door with two gas cylinders strapped to a metal trolley. Running down the charcoal carpet, the clinical battering ram before him, he roared his frustration with every pace. 'Argh!'

Inside, Felix and Granny stood slowly, fascinated and horrified by the noise.

He rammed the surgery door, it stretched like rubber. Bouncing back into place, it flung the trolley together with its load of cylinders through the air, the dead weight dragging Mr Fogg with it. Airborne, they hit the light fitting, shattering the bulb. Crashing through archway above the reception, the trolley split its load. One cylinder hurtled off down the corridor, it careered through the wall and into the toilets. The other rebounded off the plaster, shooting between Mr Fogg's still flying feet. The dentist and the trolley thudded to the floor in the reception.

Granny and Felix pressed their ears against the door. 'Do you think he's dead?' asked Felix in a hoarse whisper. A low groan came from the dentist outside.

'Unfortunately, not,' she replied.

'That's not nice.'

'Who ever told you I was nice?' she asked him.

Mr Fogg sat up. He marched to the mirror in the reception. Tiny shards of glass stuck out of his face. The lens in one side of his glasses was broken. Blood poured from his mouth, drawing back his lips Mr Fogg felt the huge hole in the front of his beautiful white teeth.

'SOUFFLEE!!!!!' he screamed. Mr Fogg shoved the empty fish tank off its pedestal, glass shattered covering the floor. Spinning around the reception, he threw chairs against walls, destroying prints, breaking windows. Mr Fogg fell heavily against the reception desk. A draft from the broken windows caught the pages of the appointment book. The busy rustle of pages drew his eyes to the name before him. Felix Van Doore 4.30.

In the dimming afternoon light, Colin and Derek had returned to the windowsill to keep watch for Felix. The alley was murky now. Shafts of light that shone from the busy kitchens windows, gouged great golden wedges out of the darkness. Derek told Colin the story of every house and the humans that lived there, as each had filled up one by one. Stories of happiness, sadness, heartbreak and joy, in kitchens before them, busily preparing dinners for families of every size. Watching people across the alley Colin noticed little reminders of life with Mrs Boardman. Families crowded round kitchen tables, homework jostling for space amongst place mats and cups of tea.

He and Granny had been alone in that tower together too long, Colin decided. For company such as Derek's he would fly with Granny, if they ever caught up with each other. He asked Derek about the Van Doore's, eager to know more about Felix's family. Ruby was busily painting herself with coloured paints set out in a row, whilst the dark-haired man sat laughing at the table. Unable to hear what she was saying, Colin and Derek watched Mum as she peeled potatoes in front of the window.

*

It was quiet, too quiet. Granny moved around the room listening with a glass against the walls. Outside an engine roared into life, lights blazed through the wire mesh covering the windows. They dashed to see. Round headlights grew smaller and the vehicle retreated. Swinging away with a lurch, the car swept onto the main road.

'Where is he going?' asked Felix, he watched the car disappear.

'Haven't a clue,' said Granny. They turned to face the mysterious door. She sprinkled green powder into the lock, and it opened with a soft click. Granny slowly pushed the door open wide.

Before them, the room was dark. A low hum throbbed in the air. 'What is that noise?' asked Felix peering into the gloom. Granny shrugged. A muscle twitched rhythmically in her eyelid. Remembering what the fairies had said, Felix stuck out his arm. 'Wait, I will go first.'

He stepped inside. As wide as the surgery before it, this room was longer. Beside him were deep cabinets with drawers. To his left was a sink, dentures and moulds were neatly lined up on little stands. He could just see the end of a silver bench, a black seated stool sat underneath.

'Put the light on' Granny hissed impatiently.

Felix rolled his eyes. 'Alright, just let me find the switch,' he whispered. Drawn to a soft light that glowed on the wall, he saw the box used to display x-rays. Looking intently at the shape stuck to it, Felix saw the delicate tracery of veins, a vivid iridescent shine sickened him. It was a single pair of fairy wings. How many times had he seen them last night, admired that magical shimmer as the fairies had welcomed him?

Felix, finding the light switch slammed his hand onto the button and the fluorescent lights flicked on. Dashing back to stand with Granny in the doorway, he turned to face the room.

Three great glass jars stood on the metal bench in a row. Scattered over the surface were instruments, pliers, scalpels, and hooks, silver dishes, and glass beakers in chaotic abundance. The jars connected by coiled wire, were each secured firmly in place with metal fixings to the neck. Felix recognised clips and copper wire.

Two mushroom shaped glass domes stood out of the jumble of wires on the first jar. The second had a huge socket attached to its lid and a third bore two shiny metal balls that fizzed with blue light between them. Granny stepped closer, the blue light grew brighter, Felix pulled her back. As she had stepped into the room the hum had changed pitch, it was Felix that would have to take a closer look.

Following the coil of wire to where it disappeared behind the bench, Felix peered into the shadows. There was a massive fuse box where bare cables dangled. How would they switch that off? In the nearest jar hanging from thin cable, Felix saw a limp fairy. Gently bouncing, she slowly turned to reveal her damaged back. Felix covered his mouth with shaking hands. Those were her wings. Dried black blood streaked her shoulders matting in ice blond hair, pooling on the steel surface it had dried into brown splodges. By the door, Granny gasped as she too saw the fairy.

'What should I do?' asked Felix. His eyes full of tears.

'Look for Nemesia,' said Granny, pointing to the other jars. 'You can do it,' she told him. He nodded, face white, tears streaming down his cheeks, Felix crept forward

With a long metal ruler Felix moved some of the tools, before the next jar. Inside, on the countertop, a fairy sat crossed legged, her shoes neatly placed beside her, she appeared to be asleep. Cautiously, Felix looked closer. The angular face had deep purple circles under her closed eyes, and full lips that were dry and cracked. Long dark hair, once neatly swept into a bun, escaped at the sides. There was a large scorch mark in the front of her blouse. Felix knew that this was the Queen, he recognised the blouse from the photos last night.

Her eyes snapped open, looking straight at Felix. They were the largest, bluest eyes he had ever seen. Suddenly a voice appeared in his head 'Release me.' Felix's jaw dropped. The sound had echoed deep inside of him, as the hum in the room had lifted its tone. Her blue eyes narrowed in pain.

'I don't know how,' said Felix. The giant eyes soaked up his, Nemesia looked to the doorway where Granny stood. 'Okay we'll try,' he said. Grabbing Granny, he dragged her back into the surgery, slamming the door. 'We can't wait for the others we have help them now.'

'They told us to do nothing.'

'No, there is no time, that one, her wings.' Felix sobbed, tears ran down his face, Granny wiped them away with her sleeve. She regarded the door that separated them from the horror inside.

'I need to know how to stop that noise,' said Granny.

'It's electricity. He has done something to the electricity box, those things on the jars they are all connected. We have to switch them off.' Felix explained, sniffing.

'And how do we do that?' she asked.

'There should be a big switch.' Felix was out of his depth now. 'That's what they showed us in Physics, but he's wired it all together, I couldn't even see a switch. We could pull them all out, but it gets louder when we get nearer, we could trip it out somehow, overload the thing. I don't know. You're not supposed to mess with electricity,' said Felix, wiping his nose on his blazer sleeve.

'How do we do that?'

'Something metal or water but it would have to be insulated,' he said.

'What?'

'Insulated, you know like, if you hit by lightning in rubber boots its better.'

'Better? You're fine, or better you don't get burnt as much?' she demanded.

'I don't know.' Felix flung himself into the chair trying to think. Filling a large glass container with water, Granny marched to the door wrenching it open. 'What are you doing, stop!' he shouted. Granny smiled then slammed the door closed. 'No!'

Boom!

Granny exploded through the door. Pieces of wood flew all over the surgery. Felix ducked, as she swept past the chair, the wellington boots on fire. The lights went out. In the darkness, Felix heard Granny land on the floor with a thud.

*

A car hurtled down the road from |Snickering, past the patrol car parked in the woods. The alarm sounded on the speed gun, waking Sergeant Blomley. Wiping the misted front window, he looked out into the darkness. But there was nothing to see, the car had been swallowed up in the dark. Blomley opened his flask and sipped his tea.

*

Felix scrambled across the floor, he found Granny in the dark. The melting rubber smelled terrible, there was a hot sticky puddle at her feet. Grabbing the thick socks, Felix dragged them off her. Weeping in fear, he scuttled to her head. 'Granny, Granny,' whispered Felix. Her head lolled, he tried to remember anything he could about first aid. Grimacing, Felix slapped her face.

'Ouch!' Granny wearily slapped him back. 'Lights,' she croaked, pulling at her belt. 'Yellow.' Felix took some powder and flung it in the air. With a whoosh, the room glowed brightly. Helping Granny to her feet, Felix guided her to the door between the

214

rooms, steadying her against the doorframe, she gestured to the bench. 'Let them out.'

Nemesia was on her feet, hands pressed against the glass that imprisoned her. He moved to the final bell jar, a fairy in red lay on her back. Felix noted gratefully, she still had her wings.

Nemesia began to glow brightly walking right through the jar shattering it, the glass pieces froze in mid-air. Growing taller with every pace, Nemesia stepped off the end of the bench, by the time her feet touched the floor, she was human sized. The glass behind her dropped to the bench with a clatter. Felix stood captivated by the beautiful woman before him, she touched his face, and his heart grew warm.

The other jars splintered and cracked, shattering, the pieces fell away from the fairies inside. Nemesia lifted Poppy from the bench, her wings draped forlornly over the queen's thumb. Whispering softly, her face glowed with relief when Poppy's wings fluttered, and she laid her gently back on the surface. Taking Primrose from the wires with great care, Nemesia lifted the fairy between her palms. Granny stepped into the room squeezing Felix's shoulder tightly, her dirty knuckles white against his blazer.

Nemesia blew softly over the body she held, red and gold sparks burst into the air and gently rose from the broken form. Beads of bright gold drifted gently across the room from the wings pinned to the light box, floating towards the queen's palms, they joined the motes that gathered and flickered brightly in a transparent copy of Primrose.

Primrose's soul hovered lightly over Nemesia's hands, turning and bobbing with a delicate elegance. Softly, tenderly she stroked the face of her queen, flitting wings the only movement between them. The fairy's body held out on Nemesia's palm faded to nothing, her luminous soul burned brighter, searing the air, and then Primrose was gone forever.

Unashamed, Felix let the tears roll down his cheeks. Exhausted, he slumped to the floor.

Lady Julia's Revenge.

Lights blazed into the alleyway. The squeal of brakes brought Derek and Colin back to the window. Beneath them, cats dashed away from the noise, diving over walls, shooting down the alley into the shadows.

'Blimey! Somebody's in a hurry,' said Derek, he strained to see the vehicle. Lights winked out, plunging the alleyway back into darkness. The golden slices of family life were the only illumination.

Colin lifted his legs to the cold pane. 'Look at them all, slinking back,' he said. One by one, the cats made their way back to the yard. With easy grace, the multi-coloured felines lined the walls, Colin noticed they appeared to be looking up towards them. A quiver passed over him. 'Turn out the light.' Colin murmured to the rat.

'If you say so.' Derek leapt from the window to the desk and turned off the lamp. Colin stared down into the dark. The cats stared back. There were more eyes in other yards, light from the houses flashed off the yellow eyes right along the alley.

'Oh my,' he gasped. 'Derek, something is not right, here.' The rat scampered up the curtains, as the cats began howling from below. A warbling guttural noise, it grew steadily, until the cat-lined alley way was an opera of feline noise. Furry faces raised up to the window, the cats sang of their displeasure.

'Let's close the curtains, shall we?' Derek suggested stiffly. 'They are taking this to another level.' He dashed past Colin dragging the case of darts across the carpeted floor. 'Bringing in that lot, it's not on.' He grabbed some knitting needles from a wicker basket by the bed.

'I'm sorry. I'm really sorry,' said Colin.

'You, what have you got to be sorry about?' Derek stopped in mid stride.

'If you hadn't saved me, that cat wouldn't have got dragged down the stairs.' Colin glanced back at the veiled window. 'This wouldn't be happening. Oh, I've made such a fuss, if I had only waited in the tower.'

Derek dropped the knitting needles with a clatter. He scurried to Colin on all fours, sitting up in front of the distressed spider. 'This has nothing to do with you at all,' he said. Smiling wistfully, Derek looked to the window, the eerie moan of the cats seeping through the thick cotton. 'Truth is, this is how it has always been, pet against pet. Dog against cat, cat against hamster, rats, guinea pigs, rabbits, budgies, stick insects, the odd snake. The owner usually thinks it's escaped.' Regarding Colin kindly, Derek said, 'Only we pets know. Aye, you spiders have it rough. However, it is not all straw beds and squeaky wheels for us either. Come on, it is time to alert everyone.'

Derek crossed the carpet to a fireplace in the centre of the wall. Clambering onto the iron grate and reaching up the chimney, he dragged out a round, fat, coloured stick.

'What's that?' Colin asked.

'This,' said Derek pulling the taper. 'Is a rocket.' Derek pointed the firework up the chimney. 'Let's have a bit of fun, eh.' Striking a match on the hearth, Derek lit the taper with a flourish. 'Take cover!' It burst into life, throwing a shower of dancing sparks over grate.

The sound made Colin crouch with shock as it shot up the chimney out into the winter evening. In a hutch at the very end of the alley, Dolly and Valentine saw the great silver explosion. With a mutual squeak, they dug deeply into the straw bedding. Swiftly, they filled plastic water guns from their drinking bottles.

*

Mr Fogg, flinched at the explosion of silver light high above the alleyway, pulling himself deeper into the shadows. At the corner of street, he watched the Van Doore house and wiped away a trickle of blood from his chin.

*

'Mr Fogg is ill,' said Nemesia. 'That man is suffering because of something you did a long time ago.'

'Oh, you are blaming me now, I didn't torture anyone,' retorted Granny 'Even now, you still defend humans.'

'I am not defending him. He is sick, made so by what you and I did. Don't you forget that.' Nemesia's voice finally cracked. Felix heard her heavy sigh. As her neat eyebrow lifted with impatience, Felix saw that Granny really did resemble her mother. Nemesia smiled lightly at Felix. 'I know that you said he had gone, but I'm going through to check.' She shrunk with a pop. Her wings flickering rapidly, Nemesia shot through the keyhole out into the corridor.

Felix jumped down from the chair. 'Look, don't sulk, please,' he said. 'We did great, but I really need to get home soon, or I'm going to be in the biggest trouble ever.'

'Yeah right, think about yourself.'

'I'm not, but we did what we came to do, and more.' Felix was hurt.

'Let's not forget, about us two. He practically tried to murder us,' said Granny dragging on the socks covered in melted rubber.

'That is not really true is it? I mean, he was out there, and we were in here. That was pretty much it,' Felix said reasonably.

'He knew my name,' said Granny.

'Everybody knows your name.'

Nemesia opened the door. 'It's safe to come through,' she said. They stepped into the devastated reception. Water rushed out of the toilets flooding the carpet. A breeze rolled papers over the shattered glass. They noticed great dents in the archway, a chair hanging crookedly from the window frame in front of the reception desk. The broken door, wide open. Behind the desk a filing cabinet, its drawers were dragged open.

'We are in so much trouble,' said Felix gawping around the reception.

'Don't worry, we will sort it out.' Nemesia was by the desk examining a page in the appointments book. 'Are you Felix Van Doore?' she asked. Granny froze, a broken picture frame in her hand. Felix eyed her carefully before answering.

'Yes?' he said slowly.

'You couldn't leave well alone, could you?' Nemesia glared at Granny.

'I didn't do anything. He brought me out,' said Granny, pointing a sharp bony finger at Felix.

221

'Traitor,' he hissed back.

'I have a feeling I know where our dentist is headed.' Nemesia said. 'You are a courageous boy, Felix. Do you think you could do me one more service?' Felix nodded. 'Then we must go to your home.'

If the dentist got to Mum and Dad first, and told them about his teeth, he would be in deep trouble. Not just 'gooseberry bush' trouble either. With the memory of his birthday still fresh in his mind, Felix knew had to get there first. 'We have to get there quickly,' said Felix. 'He will tell Mum and Dad. They will get really mad, I know it.'

'Do you have your broom in that bag?' asked Nemesia, Granny shook her head. 'Stand back!' Nemesia clicked her fingers.

Felix shuffled his feet awkwardly. 'What are we waiting for?' he asked.

'This!' Swoosh and the broom slammed into her palm. She handed the broom to Granny. With a flicker of her powerful wings Nemesia rose into the air 'Follow me.'

'Wow.' Felix leapt on the broom behind Granny. 'She is so cool.'

*

'Ha take that!'

A tight red balloon smacked hard onto the stone floor and exploded. Cats fled in terror, those hit by water yowled, limping raggedly away. In the gutter Colin and Derek rolled water bombs over the edge. Tiny squeaks echoed down the alleyway; cats leapt away from the wooden hutch in a yard at the bottom of the street.

'They're good them two!' Derek chortled. 'Always ready for a bit of action.' Sitting back in the gutter Colin surveyed the alley. Tails disappeared into the shadows. 'Most of them have gone, but she'll still be around though,' said Derek. As if answering his call, Lady Julia dragged herself onto the coal shed, her scared face aimed toward the roof. Colin cringed. it was the cat from the landing of Mr Ashton's staircase. He scuttled behind Derek as the stringy feline yowled an asthmatic warning at them. 'It's all right Colin. They don't come this far up.'

'Why not?' Colin peeped down from behind the rat.

'This is the territory of other things,' replied Derek.

'Oh, birds. Well I don't blame them, I don't like birds much myself,' said Colin, easing out from behind Derek. Out of ammunition they sat in the gutter.

'Not just birds eh? Tooth fairies, the sandman, Christmas can be a busy time as well,' said Derek. Colin was fascinated, from the tower such things were only a mere flicker in the landscape.

The lights sprang on in the Van Doore kitchen. Mum carried Ruby past the window, sliding her into a highchair, Mum gazed at the clock, Dad followed her look. Colin noticed the anxious glances both parents gave each other. Something was not right, he knew it, the clock read half past five. Then it occurred to him, elsewhere in the street children had returned from school. Where was the boy, where was Felix?

Mum moved quickly to a table and picked something up. She swung round a telephone glued to her ear, slowly the smile faded from her face, leaning heavily on the counter, she slid to the floor. Colin looked to see if the man had noticed. Slumped across the table the dark-haired man seemed to be sleeping.

'Derek, look, in the house.' Colin waved his legs at the comatose family.

'It's not very usual, even the baby is asleep,' said Derek. A masked figure strode into the kitchen. 'NO!' Colin and Derek watched as it lifted the sleeping child. With mesmerizing slowness, the figure returned dragging the sleeping woman away. The unconscious man, pulled from the table, was hauled through a door by his booted feet. 'We must get over there!' Derek was outraged. 'Let's try the telephone wires.'

Halfway across the alley, they rested on the wooden telegraph pole. Colin was anxious to get across the rest of the wires. Lady Julia gathered her troops beneath them, eager to see if the rat would fall. Derek had nothing to protect his paws from the cold hard telephone wires they climbed across. 'I don't think you should go on,' said Colin. He looked down at the cats, licking their whiskers, mocking the rat above.

'Never mind them. There are more than cats, at work tonight,' said Derek, he rose determinedly. Colin scurried forward on to the telephone wire as Derek swung beneath him, all four paws gripping tightly. They inched forward together, the cats watching intently below. Derek let out a breath, puffing against the pain in his paws. Wrapping his tail around the wire, he lifted his weight for a second. Then without warning, a violent bouncing threatened to dislodge him.

'Colin, Colin, what's happening?'

Cats had climbed the pole, they pulled on the wires with hooked claws, Lady Julia mewed spitefully below.

'Quickly,' yelled Colin, he dashed to the guttering of the Van Doore house. 'Derek, fast.' The rat heaved hard with his pink paws. The lines wobbled again. He moved only a few yards before a foot failed to grip. Flailing in mid-air, Derek slipped to his front paws. The noise from the cats below grew louder. The wire was bounced harder, Derek's left paw slipped. Colin yelled in fright. The cats below prowled noisily, rubbing each other's faces with glee.

'Hold on,' Colin pleaded. 'Hold on!' Derek winced, straining to the tips of his nail-clad paw, the cable cutting into his pads. He fell, dropping to dangle by his tail. The cats yowled, wildly pawing the air.

'Go, Colin. Save that family!' shrieked Derek. His long ropey tail started to slip against the smooth cover of the telephone wire. Lady Julia licked her lips, drooling at the sight of the wriggling pink belly.

'No,' Colin shouted, spinning silk as he ran. 'I'm coming!' He dropped a length of web silk close to the rat's face, 'Grab this,' yelled Colin, heaving he dragged the rat's paw to the wire. Hanging over him, Colin wrapped the other paw in silk. 'Now, let go and swing!' he shouted. Derek untangled his tail. Swinging crazily, Derek slid straight to the guttering.

The cats below were silent. Lady Julia eyed the pair in disgust, leaving the yard, she slunk away through the cat flap. Falling back against the slate tiles, Colin and Derek caught their breath in disbelief.

*

Mr Fogg stood in the street. Ruby slept soundly in his arms, wrapped against the cold in a blanket. The Queen would come to him, she was free, he knew by now they would have let her out. He had the child now though. Where should he go, the woods, the river? Scanning the village his eyes drawn were up to the top of the tower, as he noticed it for the very first time.

A Showdown.

They landed at the corner of the street, looking carefully about. 'Let's go,' hissed Granny. They ran silently, until they arrived at Felix's house. Granny hit something with her foot, it clanked and rolled. Curiously, she grabbed the end of an orange rubber hose attached to a long black cylinder. It hissed faintly. 'He's already been.' She wafted away the gas.

They all stared in dreadful silence at the red front door, Felix knocked anxiously.

'Mum, Dad! 'Mum!'

'Stand back,' her voice low, Nemesia pushed on the door carefully. Opening an inch, it clanked against something. Nemesia exchanged worried glances with Granny. She gathered herself, and kicked the door out of its frame, the boom echoing down the deserted street.

'The door,' whimpered Felix. 'Mum will kill you.' Granny leant in and switched on the hallway light. They crept gingerly down the corridor, drawn to the soft glow of from the living room. There in the warm light of a lamp was Dad, gagged and bound to a kitchen chair, he stared at the rat stood on his chest. Enormous dress making scissors in his paws, Derek waved at them cheerfully.

'Thank goodness you have arrived. You won't believe, what's been happening!' said Colin, emerging from Dad's long dark hair.

Mum flung her head back, as Nemesia pulled the gag from her mouth. 'Felix, where have you been? Who are you? Did you break my door?' Face flushed, Mum's eyes were bloodshot, her red hair flew wildly in all directions.

'Mum,' gasped Felix, hugging her tightly as she struggled against the bonds that held her hands together.

'You were not at Chess Club! Where did you go? No, do not tell me I don't want to know. Where were you?' Mum was hysterical.

'Mum I'm okay! I am, honestly... it is difficult to explain. But I'm okay.'

Tears rolled down her face, they fell in a deluge and then she wailed, 'Yes, but where is Ruby!'

Granny slowly pulled down the dishcloth from Dad's mouth. 'That is a talking spider, right?' inquired Dad. 'And that, is a talking rat.' Granny shrugged. Derek sat on the sofa, watching keenly.

'His name is Derek,' Colin answered. Dad's eyes shot back to Colin perched on Granny's shoulder, then to the end of her very long nose.

'Would you please put the gag back on? 'he asked weakly

'What is this?' asked Mum.

'Dental floss,' explained Nemesia as she cut it away.

Free, Mum leapt to her feet dragging Felix to her side. 'Now, I don't know who you people are, or what is going on…or…or why your nose is so big,' said Mum pointing at Granny. 'But I want to know, where my Ruby is!'

I believe your dentist has her,' said Nemesia.

'Why am I not surprised?' interrupted Bertha Van Doore. She leant against the doorframe and surveyed the scene in the living room. Bertha nodded to the Queen, 'Nemesia. So, it's your girl that has been causing problems then is it?' she asked. 'Let's go outside your Majesty, and maybe you can tell me what is going on.'

'Mr Fogg really has Ruby?' asked Bertha. Nemesia leant on Bertha's truck, she nodded wearily. 'There is something more to this, I see.' Bertha noted the deep circles under Nemesia's eyes. 'So, what do we do?'

'I will find them. The child will be fine, said Nemesia. She shook her head sadly. 'I don't know if I can save him. He has broken through the magic, done such things, all because our past.' Nemesia looked at Granny, her nose sticking out from the crowd in the doorway. 'He is not a bad man, he just...'

'Did a bad thing,' Bertha finished for her. Shrewdly, she asked, 'Do you have enough fight for this?' Nemesia nodded. 'Then I suggest you find him and do what you can. Meanwhile bring back my granddaughter unharmed and do something about her while you're at it.' They both surveyed Granny.

'I cannot change what will not be changed, 'said Nemesia. 'But if she does, our little arrangement is ended.'

'So, my prize-winning days will be over; I think I can live with that.' Bertha spotted Felix between his father and Granny. 'Felix's teeth, white by dawn?' Nemesia nodded; they shook hands briefly. 'Now where is that man?'

An explosion rocked the bottom of the tower, a bloom of rolling flame reached the top, flowering over the chimney. The wooden door, blown from its hinges, flew over the houses blazing about the edges. It shrieked with velocity, heading towards the town.

'That was our front door,' said Colin aghast.

*

In the pub, the chandelier shook, dust floated down. Kevin fell, dangling by a strand of web, he called to Old Albert, 'Looks like our Colin found her then.'

*

Along the street front doors opened sharply.

'Do not panic, it is just a rehearsal for bonfire night tomorrow. It will be spectacular!' shouted Bertha reassuringly to the faces peeping out. Doors slammed shut quickly, before anyone had to volunteer. Bertha strode to her truck calling Mum and Dad, frozen in horror, to the vehicle.

'You want to go with them?' questioned Granny. Felix shook his head

'What is he going to do with Ruby?' asked Felix. His voice was tight, great tears filled his eyes.

'I don't know,' said Colin. 'But I think we have to go to the top of the tower to find out.' Bertha beeped the horn, Mum and Dad gestured through the

232

windscreen of the truck for Felix to join them. With a determined look at the tower, he shook his head.

'I'm going with Granny,' he called.

'What are you doing, get in the truck boy!' shouted Bertha, she got out of the cab. 'Your mother is hysterical.'

'No Nan, this is my fault too,' said Felix, a tear slid down his freckled face. Wiping it away with her thumb, Bertha glared at Granny over his head.

'I swear if one hair is out of place when he gets back, that nose is mine,' she growled.

'Fair enough,' Granny drawled.

'We will block off the street, just be careful up there Felix. Don't get this wrong!'

*

At the edge of the woods, the radio crackled, waking Sergeant Blomley with a guilty start. 'Yes.' he answered the control room. It made a static noise. '.... Tow...' Crackle. '. N..... bu....' Squeak. The Sergeant banged the radio. '...explosion, at the SnickerFord tower.'

Sergeant Blomley struggled quickly out of the car. He squinted toward the tower seeing nothing unusual in

233

the village. Lights from a vehicle flashed as it moved through the streets. The tang of fire tainted the night air, Blomley sniffed suspiciously. Smoke curled white in the dark sky, seeping out of the chimney of Shuggy Mac Duff's cottage. The Sergeant shook his head sadly, about to get back into the patrol car, when a high-pitched whistle caught his attention.

Climbing a hillock, Blomley listened curiously. The whistle seemed to be everywhere, yet he could not see anything. He shivered, pulling out his torch. Hooting in the tree line proved to be an owl, amber eyes glinted before it silently swept away.

The whistle grew louder, closer, deafeningly loud. Behind the Sergeant, a ball of fire screamed toward the earth. From his place on the hillock, Sergeant Blomley watched as the flaming door landed right in the centre of his new patrol car.

*

Mr Fogg stepped onto the stone collar of the tower, a breeze blew back his hair, teasing the fringe on the blanket. Ruby moaned in her sleep. The village was laid out far below, tiny houses in neat little rows. Like teeth, he thought

Below he noticed a car, lights blazing a trail. Squinting through his good eye, Mr Fogg could make out the roof of a truck. Bertha Van Doore, he smiled painfully. Looking down at the child in his arms, he knew it would be over before they could climb up here. The Queen would do as he said, all would be well. He nodded to the child in his arms, her face a gentle round of cherubim.

Nemesia landed softly on the stone.

'I knew you would come,' said Mr Fogg. Twitching aside the blanket, he showed her the sleeping child. 'So now you must do as I wish. You must destroy the green fairy, as she has destroyed me. She came to my surgery, mine! Came to me, pretending to be innocent, using the boy. You will destroy her, now.'

'I cannot destroy Granny Green Teeth.'

'Why not? You are the Queen of the Fairies are you not?' Ruby wriggled in his arms. 'Why not?' he hissed.

'It is impossible, she was cursed long ago and must fulfil her own destiny.'

'Then, make her go away, stop the hideous creature from ruining me.'

Under the edge of the stone Granny, Felix, Colin and Derek listened. Bobbing up and down with the extra weight, the broomstick was straining to stay up.

Chancing a glance at the dentist, Granny saw him punctuate every word with an agitated footstep. Nemesia stayed carefully away; they heard her voice low and direct.

'Give me the girl Mr Fogg and I will try to help you.'

'Oh no, no, no, no... You have to get rid her or finish her.'

Granny had heard enough. 'Colin when he turns his back you, Felix and Derek get over to the steps,' she whispered. 'I want you all to stay down. Colin, check the hammock we may need more silk. Let's just take it easy and see which way the wind blows before we do anything rash.' Colin clicked, Derek squeaked, and Felix nodded.

'It doesn't have to be this way. Please, give me the child and I will do my best to help you, Arnold,'

'Arnold? My dear, I stopped being Arnold a long time ago. That eager to please doormat, what use was he, when she crept through the night stealing from me. Do you even know what she has done?' He asked her. 'Really done? I am ruined!' Ruined! How can we go back now, from all of this...?'

'Now!' Granny deposited her little team on the stone. They scurried, following Colin to the steps.

'You know what I have done, you were there. I promised to care, never to hurt anyone….'said Mr Fogg.

'I can help you.' Nemesia held out a hand. 'Give me Ruby, she is innocent.'

His mad gale of laughter echoed across the sky. 'I… I was innocent, I worked hard. Don't you see, so very hard, but she came with that boy…his teeth gone. Then everything changed, and it ruined me. Oh, yes. Do you know how much it takes to keep a family, do you? How much money it takes to throw a decent dinner party, foreign holidays? Hair, fake tans, fake nails?' With a shake of his head, he said sadly, 'How much does one lousy hairdo cost?' Sinking to his knees, he cradled Ruby in his lap.

'Mr Fogg,' Nemesia took a step towards him.

'Stay away!' He leapt to his feet, angrily stepping back, nearing the edge of the stone. 'Stay back. Get that witch here and end her,' growled Mr Fogg dangerously.

'I cannot do that Mr Fogg.'

'Then, I will drop the child,' said Mr Fogg. He turned and held Ruby, wrapped in the tartan blanket, out over the edge. Granny rose slowly from below the ledge to hover in front of him. She leant forward to look him full in the face. 'You wouldn't dare,' she sneered.

'Just try me,' hissed Mr Fogg.

Eye to eye, Granny's long nose pointed toward Mr Fogg's nightmare face. Livid bruises and beads of blood dried stood out across his cheeks, the great hole smashed between his teeth. Granny never flickered. Mr Fogg's arm trembled, and he glanced at the blanket. Her eyebrow rose in a challenge. Granny was about to reach out for the child.

'NO! No, that is my sister, don't let her go!' screamed Felix. He jumped up the stairs, Derek attached to his trouser leg. Dragging the child back to his chest, Mr Fogg swirled away from Granny. Nemesia caught Felix by his jumper.

'Felix, what trick is this?' Mr Fogg circled round the tower until he could see all of them.

'No trick,' said Granny. 'I just thought you could throw her, I could throw him, how about that?' Granny landed on the stone surface, dropping her broom.

'That is not helping Marguerite,' said Nemesia.

'Do you see, do you see that she does not care, she is evil, Evil!' the dentist sobbed, pointing a shaking finger at Granny. In the blanket, Ruby struggled awake, she started to cry.

'Please Mr Fogg, give me my sister,' said Felix, fighting Nemesia's grip. Colin dashed to Granny, scampering to her ear. A smile quirked the side of her mouth, striding towards the dentist, she swept past her mother shoving Felix hard against her. Colin leapt.

'Stay back or I swear,' threatened Mr Fogg. Backing away from them, he circled the tower trying to keep them all in sight.

'Oh please,' Granny shouted at him. 'If you're going to do it, then do it.'

'You, heartless, witch! Doesn't it bother you that you've ruined me?' asked Mr Fogg

'No,' she answered. 'Because frankly, I never cut off a fairy's wings. So no, it doesn't bother me.'

'Stop it! He will throw her, don't!' cried Felix. Ruby wailed louder at the sound of Felix's voice.

'You never liked her anyway,' said Granny, she looked at him in surprise. The others gasped.

'See, see, she's playing with your sister's life Felix,' wheedled Mr Fogg, scurrying backwards.

'Shut up!' Felix shouted at the dentist. 'She is my sister,' he said to Granny 'We did this, we went to him. He wouldn't have got her if we hadn't.' Confused tears filled his eyes. 'I don't want this. You are just as bad as he is.'

Granny looked at Felix sadly. 'Chuck the kid dentist, you are boring me now!' she said.

'Marguerite!' cried Nemesia

'Stop it!' screamed Felix wildly at Granny. 'She is just a baby!' Time slipped away and Felix heard the echo of his father's words. 'She is just a baby Felix.' His mother sitting on his bed, 'One day she will mean just as much to you.' He staggered, confused by the height and the voices, tears blinding him, he wrenched himself from Nemesia's grip, running blindly at Granny.

'Stop messing about now. Throw the kid or get off my tower dentist!'

Granny grasped Felix and thrust him away. Nemesia caught him, saving him from falling back down the staircase, holding Felix tightly, she righted them with a flap of her wings.

Ruby wailed against Mr Fogg's chest. He looked down at the child in his arms. 'No, you evil, thoughtless creature, look where you have brought us.'

'Me! 'roared Granny, striding across the stone towards him. 'Not me Mr Fogg, you had a choice and you chose this. Look where, you, have brought us!' Befuddled, Mr Fogg whirled around across the tower. He staggered, his foot upon Granny's broom handle. Under his weight, it snapped, the pieces rolling away. His feet faltering, Mr Fogg threw out an arm for balance, falling hard onto his back. The blanket was flung into the air. Out of the blanket, Ruby flew into centre of the tower.

'No!' Felix screamed. 'Ruby!'

Granny crossed her fingers. Nemesia leapt, casting silver powder over Mr Fogg, freezing his struggling body. Ruby hit the fine silk hammock, bouncing with a giggle. She bounced well, her firm little body just made for flight and the flexible silk bounced her high. Too high, the tiny child swooped in an impossible arc over the outer edge of the tower.

'NO!' Granny bellowed. That was not supposed to happen, without another thought, she leapt off the tower after Ruby.

Felix reached out for his sister, feet at the very edge of the stone. Just in time, Nemesia dived as Felix tumbled off the stone. He stopped with a jolt, out of his blazer pocket fell Derek, screaming helplessly in the air. Felix caught him by the end of his pink tail. They dangled in a breathless chain high above the village, watching Ruby drop towards the ground.

*

In the rushing air, Granny flew after Ruby. Grabbing her arm, Granny dragged the toddler towards her. 'Wee,' sang Ruby, her cheeks pink in the rushing air.

'Not right now, please,' said Granny. Holding the child to her chest, Granny reached out a hand for the broom, her heart almost stopped. She saw his foot and heard the snap all over again. 'No, no!' she cried. Granny struggled to stay on her back as their weight drove them downwards faster. Her hair streamed up, dragged by the wind that tore at her clothes. Ruby looked up from her chest, eyes wide with excitement. Granny felt a sob rise up.

'Fly, Fly, Fly,' Ruby giggled.

The sob that threatened to choke Granny, broke free. She could not bear to look. Clutching the dark head to her chest, tears streamed down her face. Above them, Felix's dangling feet disappeared into the darkness, whilst they streaked away down to the ground. Ruby lifted her head and giggled again. Granny closed her eyes against the sight of a happy child's face, the smell of Ruby's baby clean hair stifled her.

'I'm sorry,' she whispered, her voice swept away in the rush of air. 'I'm sorry, I'm sorry, I'm sorry.' Granny battled the tears to look into the innocent dark eyes before her. 'I am, so sorry!' Together they plunged toward the brick pile at the base of the tower.

'Fairy,' said Ruby, grinning.

'Yes, I am fairy' Granny smiled. Her tears flew up away into the air. A chubby finger hit her in the nose. 'Ouch, get off!' Granny gritted her teeth. Ruby grabbed her nose and a handful of hair. 'Let go of my nose.' They were rushing to their deaths; this child had no sense of occasion.

The bricks of the tower flashed past in a dizzying blur. 'Having trouble?' asked a familiar voice. Asta appeared at Granny's side, flitting under them, she grew as they dropped, wings beating hard against the rapid descent. Asta strained and they slowed in the air.

'Make it let go!' squealed Granny, they landed and flopped to the ground. Asta lay breathlessly on the pavement, whilst Granny struggled to remove Ruby's fingers from her nose. She was relieved when Mum, Dad, and Bertha rushed to them, dragging Ruby off her, inspecting every inch for damage.

Rubbing her nose, Granny tried to slip away from them, whilst they thanked Asta for saving Ruby from falling. A hand dropped on to her shoulder. 'You did a good job there, now where is my grandson?' asked Bertha.

*

Felix, at the top of the tower, sat in exhausted silence with Colin and Derek on either side. Granny staggered to the top of the stairs. She joined them wearily, and they watched the chaos below. Fairies came and took Mr Fogg away. Flitting across the village, they busily tidied away the evidence of his rampage.

'Are they really mad at me?' asked Felix. He was desperately worried about how he was going to explain all this to his Mum and Dad.

'What does it matter now?' she said.

He picked up a chipped piece of sandstone. 'Because, I'm sorry, they were right, and I don't want them to be angry with me anymore. Ruby isn't that bad,' said Felix. Big, sad, tears fell onto his school trousers. 'And she nearly... you know.' he sniffed. They all nodded. 'So, I don't want it to be like that anymore, not angry anyway.' He flung the stone away.

. 'Watch it!' A fairy flew upward, the stone in her hand.

'Sorry,' they all muttered. Colin eyed Granny suspiciously, his exhausted spider senses jangled.

'Of course, they are angry Felix, they were scared,' said Granny. Her head spun, rubbing her eyes she tried to remember what she was saying. *'Marguerite!'* She tried to look forward, but her head swam, the tower lurched. Her name echoed deep inside her. How many

244

times had it been shouted in exasperation, anger, despair? They had always been so angry. Granny clutched the stone where she sat, digging in with her nails. The pain made her focus, breathing hard, the tower stopped turning. It pitched the other way.

'Granny?' Colin touched her hand, a spark cracked between them. She looked down at him her eyes full of blue light. 'Something is happening!' He stepped away, hair standing up over his black body.

Granny swallowed, her chest was full of fire, trying to speak she gasped. Lifted from the stone, Granny started to float, blue light twisting about her body. She held out her hands, light crackled down over her fingers tips, surging back in wriggly lines up her arms.

'Quick over here,' said Colin to Felix and Derek. They rushed off the parapet as Granny started to buzz loudly, the blue light pulsing over her long thin frame. At her back, light squirmed and writhed into shapes. 'That's not right, that never happens. What's going on?' Colin was scared.

The shapes were familiar to Felix. 'It's alright,' he said. 'I think...' Felix bit his lip. Fairies across the village stopped what they were doing and looked towards the tower. A white light exploded from the sky above, hitting Granny with a blinding flash. They covered their eyes. Granny screamed dreadfully in the air before them, her voice cut across the sky echoing down the cobbled alleyways below.

Granny dropped, crumpled onto the stone. On her back, thin iridescent wings flickered in the breeze.

'I thought you couldn't change her back!' said Asta.

'I can't,' replied Nemesia. 'Although, I never said she could not change herself.'

*

Mr Fogg opened his eyes. A dark-haired man sat before him blinking politely, waiting for him to reply. 'It was always your dream to work for the charity in Africa.' Mrs Fogg indicated with her glass. 'Isn't that so, Arnold?'

'Yes? Err, yes, it is… will you please excuse me?' Sweeping his napkin from his knee, Mr Fogg stood with a curt nod. He saw a young woman to his left, with a start. Reaching the door, he looked back at his dining room, Mrs Fogg was patiently pouring another drink for the young couple at the table.

'Did you always want to be a dentist?' asked Mrs Fogg with a charming smile.

'Well…'

Finding his way to the kitchen, Mr Fogg saw boxes packed and ready to go, sealed with brown packing tape. Splashing his face with cold water, he tried to catch something at the corner of his mind. He must have been working too hard. Apparently, they were moving, he had always wanted to go to Africa.

*

They were taking down the tower, to build a library for the village. It was a good idea, decided Sergeant Blomley, especially after the fire. 'Get up,' hissed his mother. She elbowed him sharply.

Sergeant Blomley strode to the front of the village hall to receive his certificate from Bertha Van Doore. The hall was packed, and everyone agreed that Sergeant Blomley was a hero. Lights flashed; the Sergeant smiled. His picture would be on the very front of the Snickering Guardian. His memory was foggy, but he was sure it had something to do with fireworks and the explosion at the tower. Sometimes, in the night, the Sergeant dreamt of a giant ball of flames.

The Gift.

'Ruby, No!' Dad leapt before she managed to climb up the branches of the Christmas tree. It rocked dangerously, Dad swept her up and out into the kitchen. Felix squinted at the fairy on the top of the tree, who should not have cursed when the tree rocked. Getting closer, Felix recognised the screwed-up face. Marguerite struggled with the pine needles stuck in her purple wool tights.

'Do you need a hand?'

'No, I'm good thanks,' she said, fluttering down to land on the arm of the sofa. She was the scruffiest fairy Felix had ever seen. In a woolly jumper and frayed denim shorts, she wore wellingtons boots with tinsel around the top. 'Colin insisted, look.' She pointed at the tree. Hanging from a silken thread, Colin twirled. What Felix had earlier mistaken for a decorative snowflake, was Colin coated in glitter.

'Am I obvious? Is it too, Christmassy?'

'No, it's great. You look great,' laughed Felix

'You said it was too much,' said Colin to Marguerite. He clambered across the branches to join them on the sofa, 'Merry Christmas Felix,'

'Yes, Merry Christmas' she added. 'We got you a present.'

248

'Oh, but I didn't get you anything,' replied Felix. They never mentioned presents in their letter. Felix was so excited he had hardly slept since the message arrived, but he never thought about presents.

'That's all right, you have to be good to get presents. Maybe next year,' said Marguerite sheepishly. 'We put it under the tree there.' She pointed. 'You can open it in the morning.'

'Come on, let's go to my room,' said Felix. 'They won't miss me; Mum is icing the cake.'

'Well, there is the 'Naughty and Nice' list, I fill that in. I Love it!' Colin danced excitedly. 'On my own computer and everything.' Colin told Felix about his new job in great detail. 'After that, I have time to write my blog...' The three of them played scrabble in his room.

'What do you do?' Felix asked Marguerite.

She blushed, twiddling with her letters. 'Well,' she replied. 'I am a sort of assistant. I help out with some really important things for....'

'She looks after the reindeer,' interrupted Colin. 'I don't know why you are so embarrassed; they are magical you know' he said. Felix giggled, passing Marguerite a chocolate biscuit.

'I'm not,' replied Marguerite, rolling her eyes. 'It's just that they always complain, to Linden if the carrots aren't warmed properly, to Uncle Nick if the straw isn't deep enough. Rudolph is great, but the rest of them, I could tell you a thing or two. They look nice on the cards. However, they are really very selfish.' Felix and Colin collapsed on the pillows laughing, 'What?' she said. 'What is so funny.'

'Felix, Felix!' Dad shouted from the bottom of the stairs. 'Come quickly, it's starting to snow.'

He rushed to the window. 'Look,' said Felix, opening his curtains wide. Large feathery flakes of snow fell in abundance. 'That's amazing, I know you two get to see it all the time, but it never snow's in SnickerFord at Christmas.' Marguerite froze, Colin touched her hand. 'Stay here,' said Felix, grabbing a jacket from his wardrobe. 'I'll be ten minutes, I promise.'

'Felix!' said Granny. He stopped in the open doorway, shrugging on his coat. 'Hurry back.'

'Go ahead, we will wait,' said Colin. Felix rushed excitedly down the stairs.

From the windowsill, they watched them in the yard below. 'Do you think he really will forget us?' asked Colin. Marguerite nodded; a tear shone at the corner of her eye. 'I think I shall miss him very much,' sighed Colin sadly.

'Come on,' she said, rubbing away the tear furiously. 'We have to go, its better this way.' Opening a keyhole on the wall, they left the bedroom and the family playing in the snow.

In the living room under the tree, their present glowed, wrapped up in bright green paper.

Meanwhile...

From the dark, a shape burst through the clouds. Silhouetted against the belly of the moon, it swooped low over the mountains, landing swiftly in the snow-covered grounds of an ancient fortress. Toes dug deep into the soft powder, breath came in clouds and something slithered from the creatures back. 'Lady.' Shaking it's great head, the beast bowed to a figure that looked out over the valley.

'Wait here,' she commanded. Without a sound, she moved through the cobbled streets, past brightly coloured dwellings, down narrow alleys and tight winding stairs that led her through the town.

He stopped, raising the small paint brush, a last coat of gold drying rapidly on the glass before him. Lifting his head, the taste of a sound echoed through the deserted streets, speaking only to him. Quickly he rose, stepping into the office he took an envelope from his desk. Returning to his stool, he waited.

She found the door; the blind was pulled down. The large glass window of the shop front held a display of gaudy coloured globes, from within she could see the warm glow of light, and a figure that waited patiently. Pushing the door open, a little bell rang cheaply in the silence. She stepped into the warmth and crossed the wooden floor, passing high shelves stacked with toys, and glass globes that held figures frozen in time. His eyes glowed as she stood before him.

'I knew you would come, eventually…'

…not quite, The End.

Acknowledgments.

Without a shadow of a doubt, there are people who need acknowledging for their help and support in bringing this world to life.

We are without wings, but not without magic.

Sue, for your help when I had nowhere else to turn. Honest and brave, I could not have been so bold without you. My beautiful fairy tribe, Viv, Clare, Lottie, and Rebecca, your friendship, patience and humour inspired so much. Thomas who by now, must know more about Granny and Colin than I. Thank you, to the British Library and the online resources used to construct the curse. I am grateful for the expertise of our dentist, and the many friends and colleagues who have encouraged me to publish this work.

'Always let you conscience be your guide' – The Blue Fairy

Walt Disney- Pinocchio -1940

Georgiea Howarth, actor, circus artist, and brain tumour survivor, was born in Manchester. A performer for fifteen years, she travelled across the world, showing off, and collecting stories along the way. Hubris is her debut novel, and the first in a trilogy of unique tales about 'the others.' Busy mixing slapstick with mythology, into a cocktail of whiplash fantasy, she is currently writing the next chapter in, The Chronicles of a Tooth Fairy.

For more content,

www.thetoothfairychronicles.com

If you need support, or to donate,

https://www.thebraintumourcharity.org/

Printed in Great Britain
by Amazon